The Glitch

A COMPUTER FANTASY

Also by Ronald Kidd

The Glitch

A COMPUTER FANTASY

by Ronald Kidd

Lodestar Books   E. P. Dutton   New York

Library of Congress Cataloging in Publication Data

Kidd, Ronald.
  The glitch.

  "Lodestar books."
  Summary: A sixth-grade boy who hates computers
is suddenly pulled into one and finds himself in the
Computer Kingdom, where he has weird and dangerous
adventures.
  [1. Computers—Fiction. 2. Fantasy] I. Title.
PZ7.K5315Gl 1985 [Fic] 85-16040
ISBN 0-525-67160-9

Published in the United States by E. P. Dutton,
2 Park Avenue, New York, N.Y. 10016

Published simultaneously in Canada by
Fitzhenry & Whiteside Limited, Toronto

Editor: Virginia Buckley   Designer: Isabel Warren-Lynch

Printed in the U.S.A.   COBE   First Edition
10 9 8 7 6 5 4 3 2 1

to Yvonne,
with kilobytes of devotion
and kingdoms of love

Contents

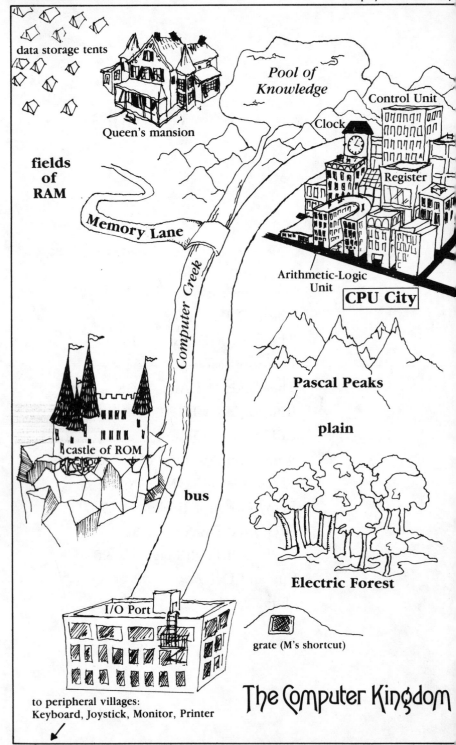

Map by Isabel Warren-Ly

data storage tents

Queen's mansion

Pool of Knowledge

Control Unit

Clock

Register

fields of RAM

Memory Lane

Computer Creek

Arithmetic-Logic Unit

CPU City

Pascal Peaks

plain

castle of ROM

bus

Electric Forest

I/O Port

grate (M's shortcut)

to peripheral villages:
Keyboard, Joystick, Monitor, Printer

The Computer Kingdom

Benjamin Bean

Kids and computers? They just go together, like milk and cookies. I look at my class, and every single child is sitting in front of a computer, having the time of his life. Yes, indeed, kids love computers.
　　　　　—Mrs. Higgenbottom, sixth-grade teacher
　　　　　Elm Street Elementary School

Look again, Mrs. Higgenbottom. See the boy at the back of the room? The short one with freckles, and a grape-juice stain on his T-shirt? He doesn't love computers. In fact, on his list of favorite things, computers fall somewhere between whooping cough and an attack by man-eating sharks.

How do I know? Because that boy is me, Benjamin Bean.

It's rough, not liking computers. Kind of like hating the circus or being opposed to summer. Most of the kids I know think computers are the greatest thing since peanut butter. They use them to shoot down alien invaders, practice spelling, move frogs across busy highways—

you name it. People say computers are going to shape the future, and maybe that's true. I'm just not sure I want to be there to see it.

My feelings are based on one simple, irrefutable fact: Computers give me the willies. No matter how much I learn about ROM and RAM and the CPU, I still can't quite believe that a glorified box can do all that stuff. Boxes are for holding cereal, not solving math problems or playing chess. Did a box paint the Mona Lisa? Did a box discover America? Did a box write "Jingle Bells" or invent the paper clip? I rest my case.

To tell you the truth, it's not just computers that bother me; it's all modern gadgets. I get nervous around hair dryers and telephone answering machines. I freeze up in the presence of digital clocks and automatic garage-door openers. I have an irrational fear of electric tooth-brushes. I'm not sure why. Maybe when I was little I was attacked by a toaster oven. Or maybe it has something to do with a grandfather whose idea of modern times was an indoor bathroom.

Okay, so if I don't like computers, what do I like? That's easy: I like the good old things. I like buggies and gas lanterns, silent movies and porch swings, washboards and black high-top tennis shoes. I like the smell of home-made bread, the sound of a steam locomotive, the feel of the wood in a rolltop desk.

My idea of fun is a day in the old part of town, exploring thrift shops and visiting my favorite place, Velma's Volumes. It's a used-book store, and everything in it is old, including Velma. It's cozy and comfortable, the last place in the world you'd expect a surprise.

So when I walked into Velma's store one summer day, how was I to know I'd get the biggest shock of my life, plus an adventure that would turn Marco Polo chartreuse with envy? And how was I to know that at the center of it all I'd find the bane of my existence—that glorified box, the computer?

It started simply enough. "Hi, Benjy," Velma called as I strolled in. "What can I do for you?"

"Write me into your will. I'll take every book in your history section, plus all the cobwebs I can carry."

"What is it with you?" she asked. "I've never seen anybody so young so old."

"I like antiques. They don't change. You can trust them."

"Thanks for the compliment."

"Actually," I said, "there is something you can help me with. I'm looking for books on King Arthur."

"Great! This'll give me a chance to try out my new filing system." Grinning, she came out from behind the counter and led me between a couple of overstuffed bookshelves.

"What was wrong with the old system?" I asked.

"This one's better. You'll see."

We turned a corner, and there, hunched over a table, was Velma's grandson Dexter, a high school student who loved tinkering with things. He looked up from his work. "How's it going, Benjy?"

I didn't answer, because I'd just caught sight of what Dexter was working on. It was Velma's filing system, and it most certainly was not old. It was a computer.

"Great, huh?" said Velma.

Yeah, it was great. Like Kool-Aid at a wine tasting. Like condos in Yosemite.

"It started out as a regular microcomputer," Dexter said, "but I added a few variations of my own." He proudly indicated a thicket of wires covering the back of the unit. "This little gem can do things you never dreamed of."

"Dexter just finished writing a program to keep track of all the books I own," Velma declared. "All he has to do is type in a subject, and this contraption spits out a list of books and where they're shelved. Okay, Dex, put this in your computer and crunch it: King Arthur and the Knights of the Round Table."

Dexter adjusted his glasses and leaned over the keyboard. "Let's see," he murmured. "Arthur, King." He tapped out a series of commands, then sat back and peered at the monitor. The computer hummed and whirred, and seconds later it gave the result on its screen: SYNTAX ERROR. "Hm," said Dexter, "must be a bug in the program. Just give me a second."

"Well," said Velma, disappointed, "in the meantime, I guess we can use the old filing system."

Resisting an impulse to jump up and click my heels, I followed her back to the counter. "Velma, do you really need a computer?"

"Are you kidding? Look at this mess." She pulled out her old files, a collection of battered shoe boxes stuffed with scraps of paper, and began sifting through them. "My guess is we'll find King Arthur filed somewhere between Nat 'King' Cole and last month's laundry bill."

"Couldn't you just straighten things up?"

"Sure," she replied, "but as long as I'm getting organized, why not do it right? Besides, computers are the wave of the future. I figure I'd better grab a surfboard before it's too late. You should do the same."

"I don't think so, Velma."

"What's wrong? Afraid of the water?"

"I guess you could say that."

A few minutes and several shoe boxes later, I had my King Arthur book. As Velma finished writing up the receipt, Dexter called out from the far side of the store. "Hey, Grandma, Benjy! Come here!"

We hurried over and found him seated at the computer, beaming. "The program's ready," he said. "I can check on King Arthur now."

"Sorry, Dexter," I said, showing him the book, "but you're too late. I'm on my way out."

"Wait a second," he begged, "you have to see this program work. Here, I'll just enter another topic—say, computers." Obviously he wasn't going to let me leave until he'd demonstrated his new toy.

"Okay," I said, "but as long as we're doing this, couldn't we at least look up something old?"

"Sure. How about the guy who invented the computer, Charles Babbage?"

That was one of the things I most admired about Dexter: his wide range of interests. I watched as he entered the name. There was a whirring noise, then once again the message SYNTAX ERROR. "That's impossible!" he cried. "I got all the bugs out—it should work perfectly."

"Dexter," I said, "have you thought about setting up an old-fashioned card file?"

By all rights, that's when I should have left. I had my exit line, I had my book, I had my quaint ideas still intact. But as I turned to go, one of life's little gremlins caused me to glance over my shoulder, and something caught my eye. "Could a loose wire be causing the problem?" I asked.

"Sure," Dexter said, getting up from his seat. "Where?"

"Here." I reached into the tangle of cables and grasped one. To my surprise, I felt an odd tugging sensation coming from the end of it, like the pull of a vacuum cleaner.

"Let's see that," said Dexter.

The suction grew stronger. It was bothering me, so I let go of the cable. Unfortunately, the cable didn't let go of me. It clung to the tip of one finger like a leech.

"Anything wrong, Benjy?" asked Velma. "You look a little pale."

I grabbed the cable with my other hand and yanked, but it wouldn't come away.

"Come on, Benjy, give it to me," said Dexter.

"I'm trying, I'm trying," I said. "Hey, Dexter, is this some kind of joke?"

"Joke?" he said, genuinely puzzled.

"What's that sound?" asked Velma suddenly.

It could have been the howling of the wind or the roar of the sea, except it seemed to be coming from the computer. It grew stronger, and as it did, so did the pulling sensation.

6

All at once, my finger disappeared into the end of the cable.

"Did you see that?" croaked Dexter.

It's funny how the mind works in emergencies. Sometimes it overloads, and you panic. Other times, it sorts things out with amazing speed and precision, leaving you with a clear view of every last detail. Me, I panicked. "My finger!" I screamed.

"Dexter, do something!" said Velma.

The cable devoured more. "My hand!" I screeched.

"Oh, my God," Dexter whimpered.

And more. "My arm! I need that arm!" I cried.

"Shut off the power!" shouted Velma, but it was too late.

With the sound of a thousand tornadoes, I was sucked into the void.

The I/O Port

I tumbled through an inky darkness, my arms and legs flailing. Sparks whizzed by. A hot wind howled in my ears. I heard a high-pitched shriek and discovered that it was my own voice. If this was death, it was a lot like a ride at Disneyland.

Up ahead, a light appeared. It grew bigger and bigger, like the lamp of an approaching locomotive, and suddenly, before I could brace myself, it was right on top of me. There was a crash, and everything went black again.

When I opened my eyes, I found myself lying on a junk heap at the end of a hallway. Nuts, bolts, wires, and oddly shaped hunks of metal and plastic dug into my back. Behind me, hanging from broken hinges, were the shattered remains of a hatch door. The rest of the door lay in pieces around me.

"Hello?" I called out. "Anybody there?" When you're nervous, it's amazing how quickly you lapse into old movie dialogue.

No one answered, but I noticed that the place wasn't completely silent. From the other end of the hall came the murmur of a crowd. I climbed down off the heap, legs wobbling, and made my way toward the sound. When I turned the corner, I stopped and stared.

It was alphabet soup gone wild. It was a typist's nightmare. It was an immense room filled with letters, numbers, and symbols. But they weren't the little black ink spots you see on a page. Oh, no. These babies had arms and legs and faces. They were three, four, five feet tall and gleamed like brand-new plastic. And colors? Izod would have a field day. There were solids of every shade, plus enough stripes and paisleys to impress the most jaded preppie.

I paused a moment to ponder how a perfectly good eleven-year-old brain can, without warning, snap like a used rubber band. One minute, healthy nerve cells; the next, tapioca pudding.

As I stood there, numb, a pint-sized letter *G* walked up. She was lavender, with blue arms and legs.

"Gee," she said in a squeaky little voice, "hello."

What do you say to a letter of the alphabet? "Uh, hi there."

She tilted her head sideways. "Gee," she asked, "what's your name?"

"Benjy. Say, could you tell me—"

She jumped up and down, clapping her smooth, pink hands. "Ben-G! Ben-G!" she yelled, and scurried off.

"Wait!" I cried, but she was gone.

Just then, a bright red exclamation point sprinted by.

9

"Excuse me," I called.

He circled back until he was facing me, running in place. "You're excused!" he yelled.

"Mind if I ask you a question?"

"Go right ahead!" he screamed, panting.

"You don't have to run and shout."

"I always run! I always shout!" he shouted. "That's just the kind of guy I am!"

"Okay, then. This may sound like a strange question, but can you tell me where we are?"

"That's a strange question!"

"Could you just tell me, please?" I said.

"We're in the Computer Kingdom, of course!"

The word *computer* hit me like a punch to the solar plexus. I could feel the sweat break out on my forehead. "Where exactly is this Computer Kingdom?" I asked, picking my words carefully.

"In Dispensable! State of the Art!"

Fighting to remain calm, I took a different approach. "Okay, what's this building we're standing in?"

"Hey, you're not too bright, are you!"

"Give me a break!" I shouted. "I'm lost!"

"I like that!" he screamed back. "You've got a good yell there! Maybe you're not so dumb after all!"

"Just answer the question!"

"We're in the I/O Port! It's where data like me and the others get in and out of the kingdom!"

Overhead, a metallic voice rang out. "Your attention, please. Program Line 20 now arriving from Keyboard. Line 20 arriving from Keyboard. Program Line 80 now departing for Monitor. Line 80 departing for Monitor."

"Line 80, that's me!" he cried. "Gotta go!"

"Just a few more questions . . ."

"Louder!" he shouted as he raced off. "Use your diaphragm! You know, if you took up running, you might really go places!" The bright red exclamation point disappeared into the crowd.

I looked around and swallowed. This place was called the Computer Kingdom, it was filled with data, and you reached it by traveling through an electrical cable. I no longer had any doubt where I'd landed. It was crazy, ridiculous, and impossible, but it had to be true.

I was inside a computer.

Why me, Benjamin Bean, the kid with the NUKE IBM sticker on his notebook? Why not Sally Goldfarb, the girl who computed the future net value of her allowance up to and including the year 2127? Why not Arnold Naze, the boy who wrote a term paper on the musical significance of the Pac-Man theme?

I stumbled forward, in a state of shock. Around me, the I/O Port hummed with activity. More announcements were made, and data of all kinds scurried about: R's rushed, D's darted, S's scampered, H's hopped, B's bounded. A grizzled period walked by, gesturing pointedly and declaring to anybody who'd listen: "Over. Finished. Done. Ended. Sayonara. Kaput." A percentage sign stood nearby, offering loans at a special rate. Parentheses huddled in pairs, whispering asides. A group of tall, thin numerals crouched in a circle, chanting, "We're number one! We're number one!"

I came to a long counter marked OUTPUT and noticed for the first time that I wasn't the only human being in

11

the room. Behind the counter were men and women dressed in neat black uniforms with the words *Port Authority* stitched above one pocket, checking lines of data through to a large gate beyond. On the opposite wall was a similar counter marked INPUT. In between, people worked at snack stands, gift shops, and insurance booths.

I spotted an information desk and was headed there when, above the noise of the crowd and the blare of the announcements, I heard a new, completely unexpected sound. Someone was singing.

Curious, I followed the voice and found a letter *M* seated on the floor, playing a mandolin and singing for a group of listeners. He wore a tattered cape, and in front of him was an upside-down beret with a few shiny coins inside.

He was green—ordinary dull green, the kind of green you see on kitchen appliances and bowling alley walls. But there was nothing ordinary about the way he sang. His voice, if it had a color, would have been gold. It would have glittered and shone like a championship trophy. More than that, it carried a sense of conviction and wonder that made you see his story as clearly as if it were projected on a screen.

The song was about a king and a queen and a love that was doomed to fail. The words were so sad and the melody so lovely that for a moment I almost forgot I was surrounded by refugees from an eye chart.

When he finished, the other listeners sat quietly for a few moments, then wandered off in groups of twos and threes. I stood watching from a distance as he got to his feet. He put two fingers to his mouth and let out a loud whistle. "Negatori!" he called. "Here, boy."

Across the floor scampered what looked like a balloon with eight legs. It was round and yellow, and its skin had the same plastic sheen I'd noticed on the letters and numbers. As it drew closer, I saw eyes that were a startling shade of blue, with a small beaklike mouth just below. But what really caught my attention was the nose. It was roughly the size of Detroit. Located beneath the mouth, on what should have been the chin, it stretched from one side of the face to the other. On the front of it was a flap, concealing God knows how many nostrils. The entire contraption jutted out over the ground, sniffing everything in its path.

The creature let out a squeak and bounded up into its master's arms. "Good boy," said the singer, hugging it close.

Stepping forward, I reached into my pocket, pulled out a quarter, and dropped it into the beret. "I liked your song," I said.

Surprised to find anyone still there, he ducked his head in embarrassment. "You're just saying that."

"No, I'm serious."

"You don't mean it, do you?" he asked.

"Sure I do. It was great."

"Really?"

"Yes, really."

"You're not just kidding?" he asked.

"No, I'm not kidding!"

"You can tell the truth, you know. It won't hurt my feelings."

"Okay, then," I said, "it was terrible."

He sighed. "I knew it."

"Hey, that was a joke. You know—funny, laugh, ha-ha."

"Really?" he asked.

"Yes, really."

"You're not just kidding?"

I felt a sudden urge to change the subject. "What's your name?"

"M, as in minstrel. I sing songs and tell stories."

"I'm Benjy, as in Benjamin Bean. I hallucinate."

He smiled uncertainly and indicated the creature in his arms. "This is my pet bit, Negatori." He placed Negatori on the ground, then picked up his hat and emptied out the coins. They were strange and shiny, the color of silver. When he came to the quarter, he stopped and examined it. "This wouldn't be yours, would it?"

"Yeah. I would have given you more, but a quarter was all I had."

He rubbed it between his fingers. "A quarter? I've never seen one before." He handed me one of the silver tokens. "Around here, we use these. They're called joules."

On it was a picture of a stern, square-jawed man wearing a crown. Above him were the words ONE JOULE; below, THE COMPUTER KINGDOM.

"Who's the man in the picture?" I asked.

He started to answer but was interrupted by the sound of distant hoofbeats. As they grew louder, the hum of the crowd died down. It was as if everyone in the room were holding his breath, waiting.

Suddenly a gate at one end of the room burst open, and a band of riders thundered in. Carrying crossbows and swords, they were covered from head to foot with armor. They rode giant barrel-chested horses, and alongside each ran a bigger, fiercer version of Negatori, every one a different color.

"The Computer Police," murmured M.

As he spoke, they wheeled and, in perfect formation, headed straight toward us.

M pulled me back into an alcove. From there we watched the lead rider separate from the group. He was bigger than the rest, and both his armor and mount were black as midnight. He reined in his horse and, with a massive hand, lifted off his helmet.

"He" was a woman.

She shook her hair free, and it tumbled around her shoulders in great charcoal waves. Her face, in shocking contrast, was as white as ivory and, except for a scar high on one cheek, just as smooth. Her eyes were black disks, and her lips were twisted into a scowl.

"This way!" she called, pointing, in a voice that trumpeted from somewhere deep in her chest. She urged her mount toward the hallway through which I had entered, and the others followed.

"You know," I said to M, trying to sound casual, "I broke a door in that hallway. You don't think they'll mind, do you?"

He gasped. "You were trying to get out?"

"No, that's how I got in."

He edged away, looking me up and down. "Joke?" he asked. "Funny, laugh, ha-ha?"

"I'm afraid not."

He looked from me to the police and back again, trying to decide what to do. "Could I make a suggestion?" he said finally.

"Please do."

"You're sure you don't mind?" he asked.

"Just say it!"

"Well, if it's not too much trouble, could you come with me?"

"I thought you'd never ask."

He eased out of the alcove, with Negatori at his heels and me close behind. We got a few inquisitive glances, but no one tried to stop us. I looked back over my shoulder just in time to see the lead rider emerge from the hallway, huddle with the others, then turn to the waiting crowd.

"Attention, all data!" she cried, her voice echoing off the walls. "A glitch is loose in the kingdom, and the King has reason to believe it might be present here in the I/O Port." M pulled me along faster than ever. "Look among yourselves," the rider continued, "and call out if you see anyone who looks suspicious."

I felt a hundred pairs of eyes focus on me, but no one said a word. Then right next to us, a voice rang out: "Here! Over here!"

The rider urged her mount forward. "Stop them!" she cried, and the other riders followed. The bits scampered along ahead of them in a great squealing wave, sniffing the ground frantically.

Abandoning any pretense of walking, we took off through the crowd. Oddly, no one tried to stop us. As we sprinted past them, some even closed ranks behind us, trying to block the riders' view. But the hoofbeats were getting louder, the squealing more shrill.

We jumped over chairs and skirted tables. As we rounded a corner and ran past a snack stand, M pushed over a food display, sending cookies and cakes sliding across the floor. I looked back and saw the bits come to a skidding halt, their noses virtually glued to the pastries. The lead rider, close on their heels, didn't have a chance. Her mount stopped abruptly, throwing her over its head into the crowd of slurping snackers. As each row of police turned the corner, they fell or jumped or crashed, until the neat formation had dissolved into a tangled mass of arms and legs.

"Follow me!" cried M. He ducked into another hallway and pried open a grill under the counter, revealing an opening not much wider than my shoulders.

"This is a shortcut I sometimes use," he said. "It's not the cleanest place in the world, and it's kind of cold . . ."

"Will you stop it!"

"Okay, okay. You go first—that is, if you don't mind, and I'll pull the grill shut behind us."

It looked a little tight, but I figured if I could fit into the end of a computer cable, I could fit anyplace. I slithered inside, feet first, and discovered after a short distance that the passage widened enough so I could actually stand up.

M scooted in behind me and was about to fasten the grill when he stopped suddenly. "Where's Negatori?"

"I thought he was with you."

We checked around us, but the bit was nowhere to be seen. "I think I should go back," said M.

Just then, we heard the drumming of hooves, and he hesitated. The sound grew louder, and the metal walls of the passage began to shake. He drew a deep breath, and his eyes took on a flat, dull look. "We'd better go on," he said.

As he moved to block off the opening, something round and yellow skittered inside. In the dim light before the grill clanged shut, I could see why Negatori hadn't been able to keep up.

Five of his eight paws were loaded down with cookies.

The Electric Forest

We stood on a hill overlooking the I/O Port, a huge gray warehouse of a building, watching as the Computer Police rode off into the distance. Behind us, set into the ground, was a grate marking the other end of our underground escape route.

"Well, what did you think of the shortcut?" asked M, with a worried look on his face.

"It could use a little redecorating. Those cold metal walls put me off."

His expression sagged. "So you didn't like it?"

"M," I said, putting my hand on what was either his shoulder or his left ear, "considering the circumstances, it was the most beautiful place I've ever been."

"You mean it?"

"Yes. Don't change a thing."

"Actually," he said, brightening, "it's not really mine. It's part of the air-conditioning system. I use it when I don't feel like getting on the bus."

"You ride buses here?" For some reason, the thought

19

of cranky drivers, hard seats, and exhaust fumes made me feel better.

He looked at me oddly. "There's only one bus, and it's not something you ride." He indicated a wide dirt path below. "The bus is a road. It's the main highway leading from the I/O Port to ROM, RAM, and CPU City."

"ROM? RAM? CPU City?" I felt computer headache number sixty-three coming on.

"You okay?" asked M.

"Yeah, don't worry about me. I'm just not used to walking around inside a metal box."

"Benjy," he said, "do you mind if I ask you something?"

"Be my guest."

"It's kind of personal."

"No problem."

"Who are you?" he asked.

It was an assignment not even Mrs. Higgenbottom would dare give: Describe yourself and the world you live in. Limit—one notebook page, double-spaced.

"M," I said, "do you ever wonder what's outside the Computer Kingdom?"

"I know what's outside: the peripheral villages—Joystick, Keyboard, Monitor, Printer, a few others."

"But what's outside those?"

He thought for a moment. "Infinity, I guess."

"Nope. It's called Velma's Volumes."

I did my best to explain, and, to his credit, M listened to me without once bursting into hysterical laughter. When I finished, I asked, "Do you believe me?"

He gazed at me for a few moments. "Yes, I think I do."

Somehow that caught me by surprise. "You do? How do you know I'm not lying? Not that I am, of course."

"I have a feeling about you," he said softly. "Almost like I know you."

"We've met? Wait, it's coming back to me. First-grade penmanship, right? Page twelve, capital letters."

"That's not what I mean. I just know you haven't done anything wrong. I know it. And I don't want to see an innocent person erased."

"Erased?" I had a sudden vision of a giant pencil chasing me down the street.

He nodded. "According to what I hear, Delete's been doing a lot of that recently."

"Delete—is that the woman in black?"

"That's her. She runs the King's debugging program."

"Why is she erasing innocent people?"

"To understand, you really have to know about the King, and that's a long story. Luckily," he said, smiling shyly, "long stories are a specialty of mine." He turned and looked down the hill. "The police could come back any time. If it's okay with you, we'd better get moving, and I'll tell you later."

"But I need to get home! Shouldn't I go back to the I/O Port?"

He shook his head. "The Port Authority guards will be watching for you. Besides, even if you slipped by them, there'd be another problem: Since you're not part of the program, you'd need an output pass."

21

"What are you trying to say?"

"You're not going to like it."

"Just tell me."

"Benjy, whoever this Velma is, it might be a long time before you see her again."

M felt that until we had a plan, our most pressing need was to put some distance between us and the I/O Port. Since we didn't dare travel on the bus itself, we were forced to take a slower route through the expanse of trees growing alongside. M called it the Electric Forest.

At first glance, the place seemed perfectly normal. But as we moved deeper into it, I noticed a strange thing: The trees glowed, almost as if there were a current pulsing through them. The glow was faint—in some places barely noticeable—but it still gave me the creeps. Lamps glow; fireflies glow. Trees don't glow. At least not where I come from.

M led the way, pushing aside branches and stepping nimbly over logs, and I followed as best I could, half expecting to get a shock each time I touched something. Negatori scampered ahead, sniffing everything in sight.

I always carry an old brass pocket watch, and as the afternoon wore on, I pulled it out to check the time. The second hand had stopped moving. The watch showed 2:05, which was the same time I'd decided to leave Velma's.

"Hey, M," I called, "how long do you figure we've been walking?"

"Oh, I don't know—eighty, maybe a hundred nano-seconds."

"Nano-what?"

"Nanoseconds. You know, billionths of a second."

I'd heard of time dragging, but this was ridiculous. "Just out of curiosity, how long between sunsets around here?"

"A millionth of a second—one microsecond."

Have a nice microsecond? Somehow it didn't sound right. There was one consolation, though. My watch wasn't broken; it was just running slowly. Very slowly.

The shadows lengthened, and M suggested we look for a place to spend the night. As we moved deeper into the forest, I heard a distant buzzing sound and asked him about it. He said it was nothing, but I noticed he picked up his pace. I also noticed that the buzzing was growing louder and that Negatori had begun to whimper.

Struggling to keep up, I pushed my way past a big tree, and suddenly the sound was right on top of me. I glanced up and saw a red-and-white blur headed straight for my face.

I ducked, and the blur flew by, buzzing furiously. I turned around just in time to see it coming back, this time chest-high. I threw myself to the ground, but in the instant before I did, the attacker's image burned itself into my memory.

If Negatori was one balloon, this creature was a string of balloons—four of them, the size of watermelons. It hadn't been flying at all; it had been swinging from the tree. The red color I'd seen was its skin. The white— well, the white was something else.

That something else was teeth.

And yet, the word *teeth* doesn't really do them justice.

23

It's like using *pistol* to describe a cannon, or *bullet* for a nuclear warhead. These "teeth," sharp as needles, sparkled and gleamed like a drawer full of diamonds. They were stacked row upon row between jaws that gaped open like the entrance to a cave. The jaws moved—back and forth, up and down, side to side—in rapid motions that produced the buzzing sound, which up close resembled the whine of an electric saw. In short, what we had here was a living garbage disposal. And it seemed that I was the garbage.

I was lying on my back, staring in fascination, when M grabbed my arm. He yanked me forward, and I stumbled along after him. I'll be forever grateful that he didn't ask permission, because in the next instant the creature swung in a low arc that carried it, grinding savagely, right through the space I had occupied just an instant before.

We crashed blindly through the bushes, going the only direction that mattered—away. The creature was close behind, swinging from branch to branch with a style that would have made Tarzan proud. Gradually, though, the buzzing sound told us that our pursuer was dropping back. When we finally broke into a clearing, the buzz was just a distant hum.

M moved quickly and wordlessly to start a fire. Only when he had a roaring blaze going did he sit down, take Negatori into his lap, and speak. "Nibbles," he said.

Granted, we were both hungry, but it seemed like a funny time to be talking about food. "You mean, like marshmallows and hot dogs?" I asked.

He blinked in confusion, then smiled wearily. "No, Benjy, I'm talking about a different kind of nibble. You don't eat it; it eats you."

"That thing back there?"

He nodded. "I've never heard of one coming out before dark. Usually they're afraid of the light. That's why I was in such a hurry to build the fire."

I looked at Negatori and shivered. "Nibbles, bits— you know, they kind of look alike."

He glanced down at his small, round companion. "Some say they're related. There are even legends of bits combining to form nibbles, and nibbles breaking apart into bits, but I don't believe them. Of course, I don't know much about it."

M reached under his cape and produced a loaf of bread, from which he tore off several pieces. "Here's dinner. Sorry I don't have anything better."

"Don't be silly, M, this is fine." I accepted it and took a bite. As I ate, though, I remembered my last meal—a baloney sandwich at home. Now, chewing on a crust of bread, sitting on the cold ground in a computer wilderness, baloney sounded mighty good.

When we finished, M leaned back against a rock. "We've got some time now. Would you like to hear about the King?"

"Sure." Anything was better than thinking about nibbles.

Nodding uncertainly, M picked up his mandolin and started playing chords. As he did, a change came over him. He straightened up, the lines on his face disappeared, and I could have sworn he turned a darker, richer shade of green. By the time he began to speak, the transformation was complete. He was a minstrel.

"Once upon a time, .003 seconds ago," he began, "the Computer Kingdom was at peace. It was a tranquil land, a neat, orderly place ruled by a monarch as stern as he was just. The King of ROM was his name, and in his kingdom, data traveled smoothly from the I/O Port to CPU City and back again, microsecond after microsecond. Everything was perfect—and that was the problem.

"The King, you see, was restless. He'd spent his life uniting small, independent circuits into one strong kingdom, and now there was nothing left to do. So he squirmed. And he paced. And he shouted useless commands to a flock of harried advisers. He was, quite simply, driving everyone nuts.

"Then came word of a princess who lived in a part of the kingdom called RAM. She was beautiful, they said. She was wild and unpredictable. The King, barely able to contain his excitement, sent for her.

"When they met, sparks flew. She was freedom; he was control. She was honey; he was steel. She was a mountain breeze; he, a thunderbolt. Naturally, they fell in love. The fact that they disagreed on every possible subject seemed beside the point.

"After a short, stormy courtship, they were married. To their surprise and no one else's, the disagreements didn't stop. The King and Queen became known throughout the land for their bitter quarrels. She claimed that he was too rigid, that he liked to boss people around, and that he refused to listen to anybody. He maintained that she had no principles, no program of her own, and would talk to any character string that wandered by.

"Finally it became obvious even to them that the marriage wasn't working. And so, unable to reconcile their differences, the embattled couple got a divorce. She returned to the open fields of RAM; he retreated to the castle of ROM, high on a rocky cliff. And they lived happily ever after."

"That's it?"

"Actually, no. But in my professional opinion, that's how the story should have ended."

"What really happened?" I asked.

"It came out all wrong. The Queen opened RAM to all visitors, and since by then she ruled her own territory, the King could do nothing about it. Instead, he quietly seethed. Finally, not long ago, came the chip that broke the camel's back: the Queen's announcement that she had expanded the size of RAM from 64K to 256K."

"The King was upset?"

"Upset isn't the word. He flew into a rage." M shook his head sadly. "Ever since, things around here have been pretty tense. First the King started complaining about lack of efficiency in the I/O Port. Then he criticized the workers in CPU City for sloppy processing of data. He even raised the baud rate on the bus, supposedly to discourage dawdling and speed up data transmission.

"Then in the middle of it all, at the worst possible time, the program crashed. The King blamed the Queen, and a bug alert was sounded. Now suddenly the Computer Police are everywhere, hunting for bugs, arresting everyone in sight, erasing data and people alike. No one knows what will happen next."

M strummed his mandolin a few more times, ending on an ominous minor chord. He stared into the fire, then tore off another piece of bread and chewed it thoughtfully.

"Great," I said. "So they're after me. Do they think I'm a bug?"

"Oh, no. Bugs are mistakes in the program—they're always data. Any other kind of problem is called a glitch."

"So I'm a glitch. And I guess that makes you . . . what, accessory to a glitch?"

"Something like that."

Suddenly I felt terrible. "M, I'm really sorry. You're in trouble, and it's all my fault."

"Don't feel bad, Benjy." He set his mandolin aside. "This may sound strange, but I'm glad we're here. In a way, I'm even glad the Computer Police are after us."

I started to make a wisecrack, but something in his eyes told me not to.

"You see," he went on, "I've spent my whole life hanging around the I/O Port, singing songs and telling stories to whoever would listen. But all that time I had the feeling I was meant to do more than that."

"How do you mean?"

"It's hard to explain. My songs are okay, I guess, but they're always secondhand. I get information from travelers and put it to music. But somehow, deep inside, I've always felt I was destined to take part in great events—

events so important and so wonderful that when I sang about them, everyone in the kingdom would stop to listen." His eyes were shining, and his fists were clenched.

"Benjy," he asked, "remember when I said that I felt I knew you? What I meant was, I think you're the person who's going to make those events happen. I can feel it."

It occurred to me that M might not stand for *minstrel,* but for *mystic.* Or *mental case.*

He leaned forward. "Benjy, something big is going to happen. You'll be in the middle of it, and I'll be right beside you."

Okay, so maybe the guy's mandolin was missing a string or two. That didn't have to stop me from liking him, did it? Especially since he saw me as the Computer Kingdom's answer to John Wayne.

"M," I said finally, "maybe you're right. But we can't just sit around waiting for things to happen."

"I have an idea. But it's probably not very good."

"Try me," I said.

"What if we went to see the Queen of RAM? Other than the King, she's the only one around here with enough power to help you. And she's supposed to be a good listener."

"You know what I think?"

He dropped his eyes. "What?"

"I think it's a great idea. And more than that, I think you're a good friend. Especially for someone I've known less than a second."

He looked up and grinned. Just then, Negatori jumped into his lap and offered him a cookie. M took it,

29

broke it in two, and gave me half. "To friends," he said. "And to the Queen."

"I'll eat to that," I replied. We popped the cookies into our mouths and chewed contentedly.

"Benjy," declared M when he was done, "I'd say this calls for a celebration."

Picking up his mandolin, he began playing a spritely tune. He rocked back and forth in rhythm, and I tapped my foot in time. The beat grew stronger with each chorus, and soon we were on our feet, stomping and clapping and whirling around the fire. Negatori scampered back and forth, screeching with delight, his nose twitching to the beat. As we danced, the darkness seemed to recede, and for the first time since I'd been sucked inside that monstrosity of a box, I felt as if things might turn out all right.

That's when we heard the noise. It was an unearthly bellow, combined with a crashing of trees and brush that grew louder by the moment. I stood paralyzed, envisioning a hoard of giant monsters bursting out of the night, and waited.

Professor Babbage

It charged out of the trees, wild eyed, snarling with rage, and headed straight for M. He took one look, and his jaw dropped like a runaway elevator.

It was a tall, frail blade of a man sporting a goatee, top hat, and scissor-tailed coat. Waving a black umbrella, he bounded through the clearing, resembling nothing so much as an angry stork.

"Music!" the man shrieked at M. "I detest it! I deplore it! I will not stand for it!" He had an English accent and a voice that sounded like the creaking of a barn door. "What's your next instrument of torture— Tambourine? Drums? Pots and pans?" With each question, he rapped his umbrella smartly on the ground. That was his mistake.

Negatori was used to sharing his turf with plants, tree trunks, and feet, but this pleated creature with the point at one end and the curved handle at the other was an entirely different matter. Squeaking with rage, the indignant bit darted out from behind M's legs, latched on to the umbrella, and with a vengeance began to pull. The man pulled back, but Negatori, showing surprising strength, wouldn't let go.

The two combatants lurched and skittered about the clearing, tugging for all they were worth. M moved back and forth on the edge of the arena, wringing his hands. "Oh, dear," he moaned. "I'm terribly sorry."

"Stop whining and get this thing off me!" the man screamed.

"Oh, yes. Yes, of course," stammered M. "No, Negatori! Let go, boy."

Finally, just as the man readied himself for one last yank, the little bit opened its mouth. The man staggered backward, pinwheeling his arms, and landed on the seat of his trousers, his top hat rolling a short distance away. Negatori hopped onto his chest and struck a triumphant pose.

M snatched up his pet, tucked it under one arm, and braced himself for another verbal assault. But the man just lay there, gazing sadly at the sky. Now that he wasn't moving, I noticed that his clothes were wrinkled and his hat bore several dents.

"It's no use," he sighed. "Go ahead, play your mandolin. Play your trumpet, your accordion, your garbage-can lid. Tell your jangly friends: The battle is won; noise reigns victorious. Charles Babbage—protector of the peace, safekeeper of serenity, curator of quiet—Charles Babbage surrenders."

"Pardon me," I said, thinking back to what Dexter had said several eternities ago, "but are you any relation to the Charles Babbage who invented the computer?"

It was as if I had stuck his finger into an electrical

socket. His face flushed, and he sat up ramrod straight. "At last," he cried, "someone knows who I am!"

"You mean you're *the* Charles Babbage?" I felt what was left of my sanity slipping away like a wet bar of soap.

What was a Victorian gentleman doing in the Electric Forest? What was an electric forest doing in medieval England? What was medieval England doing in Velma's computer? And why did my stomach hurt?

"Will someone please tell me what's going on?" said M.

"When I figure it out, I'll let you know," I answered numbly.

Regaining his composure, Babbage picked up his hat, dusted it off, and with great dignity placed it back on top of his head. "You'll address me as Professor Babbage. And what," he asked me, "is your name?"

"Benjamin Bean."

"You're from . . . out there?"

I nodded. "And getting farther out all the time."

"Tell me," he asked eagerly, "what century is it?"

"The twentieth," I replied.

"It must be glorious! Statues of me everywhere, streets named in my honor, memorials, shrines, museums . . ." His voice trailed off, and he stared into space, lost in the gleaming corridors of the Charles Babbage Hall of Fame.

Suddenly he was back. "What did I just say?" he demanded. "It was undoubtedly brilliant."

"You said there were probably statues and shrines and museums," said M, eager to contribute.

"Of course that's what I said!" Babbage snapped.

"Stop repeating me!" He turned abruptly in my direction. "You know, I always said my fondest wish was to visit the future so I could see what became of my invention. And now, here I am!"

"This isn't exactly your typical modern scene," I pointed out.

"Ah, but this is even better. Just imagine—we're actually inside a computer!"

"Yeah," I said, "terrific. Any idea how we can get out?"

"My dear fellow, I'm walking about inside the greatest achievement of my life. I have no intention of leaving."

His eyes darted around the clearing and came to rest on M's loaf of bread. He advanced on it and tore off a handful, biting into it hungrily.

"Care for some bread?" I asked.

He perched on a rock next to the fire and warmed his hands. M and I looked at each other, shrugged, and sat down opposite him.

"Of course," said the Professor, in answer to a question only he had heard, "I didn't call my invention a computer. I called it the Analytical Engine. The device itself was complex, but the idea behind it was the very essence of simplicity: If a machine such as the steam engine could be used for muscle power, why not use a machine for brainpower as well?

"It was an ingenious concept, but the public didn't understand. They laughed at me, and street musicians, knowing my contempt for their ear-splitting din, gath-

34

ered outside my house at all hours of the night to sere-
nade me. They even chased me about the city, laughing
and shouting abuse." He glanced disdainfully at M.

"I'd rather be chased by musicians than police," I
replied.

"Police? Where?"

We filled him in on our adventures, and M repeated
his nanosecond history of the kingdom, with particular
emphasis on recent problems.

"There's trouble in my computer?" bellowed the Professor when we finished. "This is outrageous! I'll see to
it at once!"

"Why don't you come with us to RAM?" I said. "I'm
going to talk to the Queen, and maybe you could check
the program for bugs."

"Precisely what I was about to suggest," he declared.
"And as soon as the bugs are eliminated, I'll start on my
next task."

"What's that?" I asked.

 • "Thinking of a more dignified word for *bug*. I'm an
inventor, not an exterminator."

The next morning we set out for RAM. As we made
our way through the Electric Forest, I asked the Professor how he had ended up inside his own invention.

"It was quite remarkable, really," he replied. "I fell
asleep one night while working on the Analytical Engine
and had a strange, fevered dream. In the dream I saw the
future, and it was filled with amazing machines called
computers, doing everything from bookkeeping to

music. Everyone was working with them—scientists, teachers, business executives. Children were even using them to play games!"

"Video arcades," I said. "Mankind's come a long way, huh?"

"And then," he went on, "I saw the most wonderful thing of all: detailed diagrams showing that this miracle machine was none other than a modern, electrified version of my Analytical Engine! All the same concepts were there, but with different names: input and output, ROM and RAM, the CPU, bus, and peripherals. Just as the enormity of it was beginning to sink in, the dream faded and I awoke."

"Back in the good old days—lucky man."

"No," he said, "I found myself lying in the forest, not far from here. When I began to explore, it didn't take me long to discover two things: Somehow, incredible as it seemed, I had actually landed inside a computer; and even more incredible, there were creatures living there who were as ignorant and superstitious as the people of nineteenth-century London."

"If you'll pardon me for disagreeing, Professor," said M, "I don't think it's fair to say we're superstitious. It's just that we believe in Logic."

The Professor looked at him with the kind of expression you'd get if your dog began reciting the Dow Jones averages. "My dear fellow," he said, "that's the most encouraging thing I've heard since I arrived here."

"It's true," said M. "The High Priests of Logic are the most respected and feared citizens in the kingdom."

The Professor's face turned red, and for a moment I

was afraid he might eat his umbrella. " 'The High Priests of Logic'? Ye gods, they've turned logic into a religion!"

M cringed but held his ground. "Excuse me, sir, but it's well known that the mysterious force of Logic runs the entire kingdom. It's so powerful that it can change a plus into a minus or an *A* into a *Z*. Don't you think that that deserves worship?"

"I think nothing of the kind!" sputtered the Professor. "Logic is nothing more than clear thinking. In a computer, it's simply the mechanism for handling data." He turned to me, shaking his head. "Most unscientific, don't you think? And in a computer, of all places!"

"Professor," I said, "I've got a confession to make: I've never been very big on science myself."

"Don't be ridiculous. You're from the age of computers."

"I'm not too crazy about those, either."

He stared at me, incredulous. "Why not?"

"I guess I think they're doing things that people should do for themselves. It may sound corny, but computers don't leave much room for things like imagination and dreams."

"But that's *exactly* what they do!" he exclaimed. "By handling the job of data processing, they free our imaginations to soar to glorious new heights."

I shook my head. "Sorry, Professor, I can't see it. The only job I'd like the computer to handle is getting me home."

The Fields of RAM

Early that afternoon we came to the edge of the forest. M picked up Negatori and turned to us. "For the last part of the trip, we'll have to travel on the bus. There's no other way to reach RAM."

"Ah, yes, the bus," declared the Professor. "It's the computer's main communication avenue—the route along which data travel from the I/O Port to the rest of the computer. Splendid, don't you think?"

"It may be," replied M, "but it's deserted during bug alerts. If the Computer Police come along, we'll be sitting ducks."

"Running ducks," I corrected him.

Checking right and left, we stepped cautiously onto the bus. It was nothing more than a wide dirt road with a broad plain on one side and a stream called Computer Creek on the other. We walked along, with M watching the road ahead, the Professor checking behind, and me scanning both sides, swiveling my head like a referee at a tennis match. By midafternoon I noticed that the flat plain had given way to low foothills, beyond which lay a range of rugged mountains. I asked M about it.

"That's Pascal Peaks," he explained. "It's said they're populated by a strange race of data so backward that they can't even speak the King's BASIC. Can you imagine?"

"Yeah," I said, "and I'm getting better at it all the time."

Nighttime was approaching when we left the bus, crossed a bridge over Computer Creek, and headed up a trail called Memory Lane, toward the entrance to RAM. Tired from a long day of travel, we made camp behind a row of elms. The prospect of seeing the Queen the next day was almost enough to make me forget I was walking around inside a world that had a plug, warranty, and instruction manual.

The next morning Negatori found a blueberry bush, and we had berries for breakfast. We set out shortly after that and soon found ourselves on top of a hill, peering down at the fields of RAM. They stretched as far as the eye could see and were crowded with people and thousands of data, giving the place the appearance of a huge living quilt. A banner was draped between two trees.

Now Entering RAM, it proclaimed. Bytes Free: 64K.

"Wow, free food," I said. "Too bad we just ate."

We descended into RAM. As we drew closer, the place took on a carnival air. Like the I/O Port, there were crowds of data and people to handle them. But here, no one seemed in much of a hurry to get anyplace —they were too busy having fun.

39

Vendors sold pretzels, lemonade, and candied apples. There were booths featuring everything from ringtoss to darts. Wandering through it all were data like those I'd seen before and lots of new ones. C's ran around in baggy outfits, playing pranks and squirting each other with seltzer water. A's formed human pyramids and did tumbling stunts. J's kept four, five, six brightly colored balls in the air at a time.

"I don't want to seem like a grouch," I said, "but since this is a computer, shouldn't these data be working?"

"Why?" asked M. "In RAM, there's nothing to do."

"To be more precise," the Professor said, "RAM, or Random Access Memory, is the part of the computer where incoming data are stored before being processed in the CPU. They have nothing to do but wait; there is no work as such."

We moved forward into the crowd and were approached by a blue-and-yellow plaid asterisk carrying a briefcase. "You look like my kind of folks," he said, flashing a toothy grin, "so you know what? I'm going to give you a special deal on a rental."

"What are you renting?" I asked.

"Me, of course! Why spend money on a big house, expensive clothes, and fancy jewelry, when for just a fraction of that cost you can rent an asterisk? With me beside you, people will know you're important. What do you say, folks?"

The Professor shot him a withering glare, and he hurried off.

A little farther on, between the mime troupe and the brass band, we were stopped by a question mark wearing a bow tie and straw hat. "Want to hear something funny?" he asked, elbowing me in the side. Without waiting for an answer, he turned to his buddy, a quotation mark sporting an identical outfit. "Hey, Mark," he said, "what do you think of RAM?"

"Well, Mark," he answered, "I think it's a pretty 'fair' place." They shrieked with laughter.

The question mark winked at us. "Say, Mark," he went on, "why don't you climb to the top of Pascal Peaks?"

"Gee, Mark," he replied, "that's a 'tall' order." They howled.

"Haven't I seen you someplace before?" said M.

"Ever watch those late-night variety programs on the monitor?" asked the question mark.

"Wait, I've got it," exclaimed M. "You're the Marks Brothers!"

"Right on the 'mark'!" said the quote.

"What took you so long?" asked the other.

"I didn't recognize you without your third brother," M said. "Let's see now, what was his name?"

"Mark," said the quote. "What a pair he and I made. We debuted in a word-processing program, then met up with Mark here and, well, you know the rest. Overnight, we were the 'hottest' act on the talk-show circuit."

"So what happened?" asked M. "Where is he?"

"He ran out on us—vanished into 'thin air.'"

"Can you believe it?" his brother said. "Right after we'd just signed that big network deal?"

"What are you going to do?" I asked.

The quote shrugged. "Just 'mark' time till he shows

up again. Luckily, we landed this gig in RAM, but let me tell you—after appearing on the monitor, it's tough being a lounge act."

"Say, Mark," said his brother, "is it true you have a birthday coming up on the twenty-third?"

"No, Mark," he answered, "you've got the wrong 'data.'" Whooping with laughter, they went on their way.

Wandering around on our own didn't seem to be getting us anywhere, so we started looking for someone in charge and came upon a group of men lounging under a tree. They wore matching uniforms with RAM insignias on their lapels, but their manner was anything but soldierly. They were joking among themselves, tossing dice.

"Excuse me," I said. "Can you tell us where we could find the Queen?"

A few of the men looked up. One of them, a grinning redhead, answered, "Have you tried her mansion?" He directed us to a stand of trees not far away, behind which he said we'd find the Queen's house and something called the Pool of Knowledge.

The Professor, who seemed agitated, declared, "Gentlemen, I must say I find your behavior most unseemly. I think your commanding officer would be very interested to hear that his soldiers are gambling on duty."

Chuckling, the redhead answered, "In the first place, we're not soldiers; we're the Queen's guard. And in the second place, I'm the commanding officer. They call me Laughalot."

"If you're the Queen's guard, why aren't you with her?" asked the Professor.

The man seemed to think that was funny. But then, he seemed to think everything was funny. "She hates it when we stay too close to her. Says it reminds her of ROM."

"It sounds to me as if this ROM must be a fine place," the Professor snapped.

For once, Laughalot didn't smile. "If you'd ever been there, you wouldn't say that. Just pray to Logic you never have to go."

We left them to their game and hurried on. Sure enough, behind the trees were the Pool of Knowledge and the Queen's house. The "Pool" was misnamed; it would take a good day's walk just to get around to the other side. Perched on its shore was the house, a dilapidated Victorian mansion. Somehow it reminded me of Velma, and I found myself thinking that if everything went according to plan, I'd be seeing her again soon.

The front door yawned open, so we went inside. We crossed into the drawing room, and there, fast asleep, with a dead cigar in his mouth and his feet propped up on a table, was a murky green dollar sign.

The Professor rapped his umbrella on the table. The dollar sign's head jerked back, and two bloodshot eyes popped up like the totals on a cash register. He jumped to his feet and grabbed the cigar from his mouth. "Well, well," he said, "look what we have here—customers!"

"Actually," I said, "we were looking for the Queen."

"She's in the study. Five joules, please."

"That's ridiculous!" the Professor said.

"That's life," replied the dollar sign. "What'll it be—cash, check, or credit card?"

"Let me get this straight," I said. "The Queen charges five joules for visits?"

"Are you kidding?" he said. "That's just for the information. The visit itself will run you another thirteen fifty."

"Outrageous!" said the Professor, and turned to go.

"Three joules, exit fee," said the dollar sign. He held a match to his cigar, puffed a few times, and blew a smoke ring toward the ceiling. "Let's see—so far, we got eight joules if you go or twenty-one fifty if you pop for the royal visit."

"Wait a second," I said. "How do we know you even work for the Queen?"

"You think I'd stand here collecting money in the Queen's house without her permission?" he asked, brushing himself off. Clearly, he was offended. Just as clearly, he was edging toward an open window.

"Need some fresh air?" I asked.

He broke into a run, took a flying leap, and was out the window faster than last week's allowance.

"I'd go after him," I said, "but my mother told me never to chase after money."

Eager to see the Queen, we headed for the study. It was empty. So were the banquet hall, the kitchen, the library, and the remaining forty-two rooms.

And all at once, faced with the prospect of spending the rest of my life inside a computer, so was I.

Run for Your Lives!

We left the mansion and went to look for the Queen in nearby data storage. Consisting of row upon row of tents, it was the part of RAM where programs stayed while waiting to be processed.

I'd heard the expression *256K RAM* and knew that it indicated RAM had room for 256 kilobytes (over 256,000 bytes) of data. But until that moment, I hadn't realized what it really meant. Imagine the Rose Bowl with the Astrodome right next to it and Yankee Stadium next to that. Pack all three with sports fans. Then give each of those fans a tent, and tell them to spread out. That'll give you some idea of what we were up against. Trying to find the Queen there was like looking for a needle in a whole field of haystacks.

After visiting several hundred tents, M and I gave up and decided to return to the carnival grounds. The Professor wanted to stick around and check the program for bugs, so we agreed to split up and meet later by the Pool of Knowledge.

As M, Negatori, and I crossed through a woodsy area, M stopped suddenly. "Did you hear that?" he asked.

Through the trees came a faint melody, shimmering like a spider web in a rainstorm. "It's nice, M," I said, "but don't you think we need to get going?"

"Couldn't we at least stop to see who's playing? If it's another minstrel, we might get some news of the Queen. Besides, the music is so pretty."

The fact was that I owed M, and this was the first favor he'd asked of me. "Okay," I said. "Lead the way."

We stepped off the path and followed the melody down a slope and into a glade. There beneath a tree sat a woman playing a small wooden harp. She wore sandals and a simple peasant's dress. On her long blonde hair was a wreath of daisies. Her eyes were green, and her skin had a pale, almost translucent quality. When she saw us, she smiled, and the place lit up.

How do you measure beauty? The Professor would probably take the scientific approach, using some gizmo he'd built out of nuts, bolts, and coat hangers. Me, I'm not so scientific. I use the Katie Rosenbloom scale.

Katie Rosenbloom is a girl in my class at school. She's got pretty features, sure. But what makes her beautiful is the way you feel when you're around her. When she walks into a room, it's like somebody threw open the curtains and flooded the place with sunshine. That's how I felt when this woman smiled. On the Katie Rosenbloom scale, she scored 110, easy.

Obviously I wasn't the only one who'd noticed. M was standing as still as a rock, his eyes glazed, looking as if he'd heard a bomb blast through a stethoscope. Whatever method he used to measure beauty, the needle had just gone off the scale.

Not even Negatori was immune to it; he scurried over and rubbed against the woman's legs. She scratched his head and said to us, "I just love bits, don't you?"

M nodded dumbly.

I shrugged. "I'm more of a dog person."

"Are . . . you a minstrel?" M finally managed.

"Not far off," she answered. "I'm a gypsy."

"Your music was wonderful," he said, with a vague smile on his lips. "Would you play some more?"

We needed information, not music. But somehow, watching M, I couldn't bring myself to say anything.

"I'd love to," the woman said, "if you'd accompany me on your mandolin."

"Mandolin? You mean this?" She nodded. Dazed, he took the instrument from his shoulder and strummed a few chords. Then he gestured for her to start.

It was a haunting melody that swooped and swirled under her fingertips. M listened for a while, then joined in with steady, pulsing chords in a minor key. Several bars later, the woman began to sing.

The song was about a place of high magic—a temple or shrine of some kind where data went to worship. The words spoke of data being transformed, and it took me a few moments to realize that the transformation was more than your usual conversion experience. It was an actual physical change. *B*'s became *C*'s, 3's became 4's, commas became apostrophes. The song described dark figures in long, flowing robes who loomed over the scene, their faces obscured.

M joined in the second time through, singing harmony to the woman's strong lead. Their voices blended perfectly, and there was a oneness about their phrasing that made it sound as if they'd been performing together all their lives. As I watched the glow on their faces, I thought of my Saturday morning piano lessons and silently vowed that if I ever got home, the first thing I'd do would be to practice my arpeggios.

They finished the song and smiled at each other. "Lovely," said the woman.

"Perfect," murmured M.

"I hate to spoil the mood," I said, "but, M, aren't you forgetting something?"

"Yes, of course," he replied. "Madam, thank you from the bottom of my heart."

"I was thinking of the Queen," I said. "Aren't we going to ask about her?"

M blinked a few times, as if coming out of a trance. "Hm? Oh, I'm sorry, Benjy."

"Is anything wrong?" asked the woman.

Before I could stop him, M had launched into his version of my life story. I had to admit, the guy was a real pro. By the time he finished, he had me sounding like a cross between Jonah and Luke Skywalker.

"And you think the Queen can help you?" the woman asked me when he was done.

"I'm sure hoping so."

"You know, Benjy," she said, "I've always believed that the first place to look for help is within yourself."

"I tried that. The only thing I found was a baloney sandwich."

"Don't be so sure. You may have resources you've never used." She set the harp on the ground next to Negatori, opened a hand-stitched bag, and pulled out what looked like a gleaming white bowling ball without the holes. She placed it on her lap and began caressing it, humming softly as she did.

Now, I like bowling as much as the next guy, but let me tell you, this was weird. It was like the ball was a friend of hers—a very close friend. I was about to look away when suddenly the white surface of the ball began swirling like fog in an ocean breeze. The fog lifted, and the woman was staring into a transparent globe.

I'd never been big on fairy tales, but I'd heard enough of them to know what I was looking at. It was a crystal ball.

"Pardon me," I said, "but if you don't mind my asking, what do you see in there?"

"Your future." She peered into the globe, her green eyes glinting. She nodded slowly. Then, almost too quickly to see, something flickered across her face. It was a look, a feeling. She tried to hide it, but she was too late.

It was dread.

A frigid breeze began to blow, and with it came the sound of horses, pounding through the woods toward us. Before we could move, a phalanx of riders broke into the clearing. Laughalot and the Queen's guard galloped up, with weapons drawn and faces grim.

Instinctively, M moved in front of the woman, and I joined him. "What do you want?" M asked them.

49

"Out of our way!" Laughalot said.

"If you're looking for someone to bother," I said, "why don't you go find the Queen?"

"This *is* the Queen," he replied.

We gaped at the woman, and she shrugged. "I hate it in that dusty old mansion, so I decided to put on this disguise and go into hiding. I can keep track of things better this way, and besides, it's more fun. I hope you don't mind my tricking you."

I said, "Then if you're the Queen—"

"My Lady," Laughalot broke in, "we've come to report trouble. The Computer Police have burst into RAM without permission and are searching for bugs and glitches."

"Where are they now?" she asked.

"Right behind us," he said. "They'll be here any moment."

"Benjy," said M, "maybe we should go."

"We can't go! She's my ticket home. Besides, they can't hurt us when we're with her."

"Your Highness," said Laughalot, glancing nervously over his shoulder, "please—"

She stopped him with a flick of her wrist, then turned to me. "Benjy, there are different kinds of power. The King has one kind, and I have another. I'm afraid I can't protect you from the Computer Police."

"Then get me out of this stupid computer! Snap your fingers, wave your wand, do something!"

She shook her head. "I'm sorry, Benjy. You must rely on yourself. And your friends."

"Well," I said, "it's been swell. Come on, M."

He scooped up Negatori, then hesitated, knelt quickly in front of the Queen, and kissed her hand. Rising, he hurried with me into the woods, but not before I'd caught a glimpse of something in the crystal ball.

I could have sworn it looked like a dragon.

We raced through the undergrowth. The cold wind whipped the tree branches in our faces, but we barely felt a thing. A moment later, we emerged next to the mansion. The Pool of Knowledge lay before us, and on the shore stood the Professor. "Hurry!" he called, waving frantically.

Breathlessly he explained that when he had seen the Computer Police, he'd hurried to our rendezvous point and devised an ingenious means of escape. "There!" he proclaimed, gesturing triumphantly.

Lying on the ground, cracked and battered, was the front door to the mansion.

"I took it off its hinges and dragged it down here," he said. "It should work very nicely, don't you think?"

"What are we supposed to do?" I said. "Knock on it?"

"No!" he bellowed. "We're going to float to the other side of the lake. Now come on, help me get this thing into the water."

I was about to point out that it might not be big enough for the three of us when I heard hoofbeats and shouts. Without a word, I grabbed one end of the door, and the Professor grabbed the other. M placed Negatori on top, then helped us lift. We set it on the lake and waded out until we were nearly waist deep. The wind had picked up, making the surface of the water choppy.

I scrambled up onto the door, and as I helped the

others pull themselves aboard, Delete and the Computer Police rode out from behind the trees. That was when it hit me.

"Professor," I said, "you forgot one small detail."

"And what, might I ask, is that?" he asked, heaving himself up on the wooden slab.

"How do we get this thing to move?"

He climbed unsteadily to his feet. "We'll use the laws of physics, of course."

"I hope they're shaped like oars," I said.

He opened his umbrella and held it out behind him. The wind caught it, and slowly the door began to move toward the middle of the lake. "The principle of force acting on an object," he declared. "Elementary physics."

On shore, the Computer Police loaded their crossbows. There was a *plop* as something hit the water several feet away.

The Professor glanced back toward the police, then at M. "Your cape," he said. "Stand up!"

M struggled to his feet and spread his cape. As he did, an arrow quite suddenly sprouted next to Negatori. The little bit squeaked, lost his balance, and tumbled over the side.

"Negatori!" cried M.

"Don't move!" the Professor shouted. "Keep your arms up!" He held the point of his umbrella out over the water. Negatori, thrashing wildly with all eight legs, was just beyond its reach.

"Benjamin," barked the Professor, "take my hand and brace yourself. Quickly now!" I clasped his hand firmly in one of mine, and with the other I took hold of the big brass door handle. As arrows rained down around us, the Professor leaned slowly forward until his body was almost entirely over the water. Negatori disappeared under a wave, then came up again, gurgling, and chomped down on the tip of the umbrella.

"All right, Benjamin, pull!" the Professor said. I did, finding strength I never knew I had. A moment later, Negatori was back on board, dripping wet but safe and sound, thanks to the Professor and—of all things—the pleated monster Negatori had attacked just a short time before.

M, his eyes shining with gratitude, started to say something, but the Professor waved him off. "Ridiculous little beast," he growled, resuming his stance at the end of the door.

Slowly we picked up speed. There were fewer and fewer arrows. The cries on shore receded into the distance, and soon we were alone with the wind and the whitecaps.

CPU City

It was early afternoon when we landed on the far shore of the Pool of Knowledge. I hopped off our makeshift boat, with Negatori at my heels and the others close behind.

By all rights I should have been discouraged, having gotten no help in RAM. Instead, I felt a kind of manic energy. After all, the Queen hadn't told me I'd never get home; she'd simply said I would have to arrange the trip on my own. At least that was the way I chose to interpret it.

"Okay, guys, what next?" I said.

"I suppose we could try CPU City," M replied. "It's where they handle the everyday affairs of the kingdom. And I think they keep records."

The Professor perked up. "Perhaps there are documents regarding the bug."

"They also issue output passes," offered M.

"Now you're talking!" I said. "Where is this place?"

"A microsecond's walk from here."

"Then we'd better get going," I said. "Delete and her buddies can't be too far behind."

We followed a seldom-used path that took us through a range of mountains. As we walked, the Professor pontificated. He described his other inventions, which included the cowcatcher, a submarine, an earthquake detector, a method for picking locks, and a technique for deciphering codes. Somewhere between the cows and the codes, we stopped for the night.

Early the next morning, we came upon a magnificent view of the Computer Kingdom. Behind us was RAM, with its hodgepodge of activity, its Pool of Knowledge, and its rows and rows of tents. We saw the bus winding off in the distance, bordered by Computer Creek and the Electric Forest. Looming over it all, crouched atop a rocky cliff like a spider preparing to strike, was the castle of ROM.

Stretched before us in the other direction was an even more remarkable sight. I knew what it was, because I'd seen pictures of it on Mrs. Higgenbottom's bulletin board. It was a computer chip.

Have you ever seen those computer ads where somebody's holding a chip on the end of his finger? Well, all I can say is, perspective sure changes things. In the Computer Kingdom, that tiny chip was a huge metropolis, and its intricate web of circuits was an immense grid of streets and buildings and gleaming towers, perfectly precise and symmetrical, rising high into the air.

We gazed out over the valley. "CPU City," murmured M.

I nodded. "The Big Chip."

"A triumph of rationality," said the Professor. "You'll hate it, I'm sure."

We descended the trail to the city's edge, where the view was even more spectacular. Besides the cleanliness and order of the place, the thing that impressed me most was its sheer size. Streets and buildings stretched endlessly left and right, and the towers—well, they towered. There was just one thing missing: people.

We made our way down the deserted streets, resisting the impulse to tiptoe. As we turned a corner, the silence was suddenly shattered.

When I think of chimes, I've always pictured little jingly things that blow in the breeze or melodic bells that play when somebody comes to your door. No longer. For me, chimes will never be the same.

They exploded like a twenty-megaton bomb from the tower of the building next to us, lifting us into the air, shaking us like rag dolls, and throwing us to the ground, where we sat, stunned.

And then an amazing thing happened: Doors opened, and people streamed out. Before you could say "Central Processing Unit," the streets were jammed with pedestrians—thousands of them, hurrying as fast as they could go. Even more amazing was the way they looked: All of them, men and women, had identical pin-striped suits, black briefcases, and nervous frowns.

I got the creepy feeling I'd somehow stumbled into a bank president's nightmare.

We jumped to our feet, having no desire to be trampled. Then, with M carrying Negatori, we pushed our way to the chime building, wedged open the door, and slipped inside.

We were in a lobby of some kind. Like everything else in CPU City, it was immaculate. There were a few simple chairs, a desk, and not much else. The room's most striking features were its high ceiling and the spiral staircase that wound down from it.

We watched through the door as the crush continued. Then, as suddenly as it had started, it was over. The street was empty once again.

"Could somebody please tell me what just happened?" I said.

Before anyone could answer, there was a hollow click, then another. Someone was coming down the stairs, but because of our low angle, we couldn't see who it was.

"Hello?" I said in a wobbly voice. There was no reply. The clicks continued, growing closer now.

"This is absurd," said the Professor. He strode across the room and rounded the bottom of the staircase, brandishing his umbrella. "See here—"

He stopped abruptly, eyebrows raised, then stepped forward and offered his arm. Out from behind the staircase came an elderly woman in a pink chiffon party dress. She took the Professor's arm and walked toward us.

"Welcome to the Clock," she said, smiling. "I'm Mother Time."

"Why didn't you answer when I said hello?" I asked.

Her answer was no answer, which gave me my answer. You've heard of people having a ringing in their

57

ears? This was the classic case. She could barely hear a thing.

Raising our voices, we introduced ourselves and explained that we were new in town.

"I just love visitors," she said, "but around here everyone's too busy to stop by. If you're not in a hurry, come on upstairs, and I'll show you my office."

We followed her up the staircase into a room similar to the first, with one big exception: clocks. There were hall clocks, wall clocks, big clocks, little clocks, pendulum clocks, digital clocks, and every other kind of clock you've ever seen. But instead of having twelve numbers on their faces, these clocks had ten. I remembered what M had told me about time in the Computer Kingdom and guessed that the ten numbers had something to do with nanoseconds and microseconds.

"You have quite a collection of clocks," I said.

"Rocks? Good gracious no, dear, I'm more interested in timepieces. It's my job, after all. You see, I keep track of time for the whole Computer Kingdom. Every one hundred nanoseconds, I go up to my bell tower"—she gestured toward a second stairway leading upward—"and ring the chimes. Of course, you may not have noticed."

"Now that you mention it," said the Professor, "I do seem to recall a faint tinkling sound."

"When I started this job," Mother Time went on, "I had just one clock. Then I began to think: What if it stopped? So I got another one. But two clocks can also stop, so I got still another. Now look at me. I've got one of every kind of clock ever made. As I like to say,

I've got all the time in the world." She tittered merrily.

I pulled out my pocket watch. "Here's one I bet you've never seen. Want to look at it?"

"Pardon me," she said, "but I couldn't help noticing your watch. Would you mind if I looked at it?" I handed it to her.

"Of course," she said, examining it, "with twelve numbers it's quite useless, but I must admit that it has a certain style. Would you consider selling it?"

"Sorry," I said, taking it back, "but I'm hoping I'll need it again someday."

"Which brings us to the reason for our visit," shouted M. "Could you tell us where output passes are issued?"

"Gladly," she replied. "In fact, I'll give you a little tour of CPU City." She led us to her desk and spread out a map. "Here we are, in the Clock," she said, pointing a dainty finger.

The Professor nodded sagely. "The pulse of the computer. It sends out regular signals by which all the computer's activities are timed."

"Over here," she continued, "is a monastery called the Arithmetic-Logic Unit. It's run by the priests of the Logical Order."

"Monastery, indeed," scoffed the Professor. "It's the brain of the computer, where data are changed by means of simple logical operations."

I remembered M's song describing the place of high magic and noticed that he was shifting uncomfortably. The Professor's remark didn't bother Mother Time, though, because she hadn't heard it.

"Right here," she said, gesturing, "is the Register. Cute little hotel—you may have seen it."

"Temporary storage," said the Professor. "It's where data are kept while awaiting processing."

"And finally," she said, "here's the place you're looking for: the Control Unit. You can't miss it because it's the tallest skyscraper in town."

"Ah, yes," said the Professor. "It controls and monitors all operations of the computer."

She glanced at a clock. "Uh-oh. It's almost time for me to ring those chimes again."

"Well," I said quickly, "this is where we came in. If we get a chance, we'll stop by again later."

"All right, then," she replied, smiling. "And, say, if you get a chance, why don't you stop by again later?"

Wendell the Wild Man

The woman behind the counter wore a suit and a nervous frown.

"Hey, finally, a real individualist," I said. "No brief-case."

She pulled a stack of forms from under the counter and handed one to each of us. "Fill these out, please."

Thanks to good directions from Mother Time, we'd located the Control Unit building and had gone inside its lobby, an imposing room of metal and glass. The minute we walked in, we realized what had happened to the street crowds that had so mysteriously disappeared. They hadn't gone away; they'd just gone inside, where they were busy carrying reams of paper, piles of paper, armloads of paper.

"What's this for?" I asked, taking a form from the woman. "We haven't even told you what we want."

"It's an entry questionnaire. Everybody has to fill one out."

I looked it over. " 'Monthly consumption of artichokes'? 'Number of encounters with left-handed chess players'? 'Surface area of toenails'?"

"We need detailed records on every visitor. I'm sure you understand."

"What if we don't know the answers?" asked M.

"Just take a guess."

After completing the forms, we explained that we needed an output pass, and she directed us to an office on the thirty-seventh floor. While we waited in a crowd for the elevator, M edged closer to the Professor and me.

"I don't want to upset anybody," he murmured, "but that security guard is staring at us."

I glanced over at the guard just in time to see him go inside an office and close the door.

We took the elevator, which was apparently designed by the same guy who invented sardine cans. When we got off, we found ourselves being swept down a mazelike corridor on a tide of wing tips and lapels. We were finally dumped at the end of the hall like so much tangled seaweed.

"Anybody know where we are?" I asked, dazed.

"Yeah," said M, holding Negatori close and looking around. "Lost."

"That's easily remedied," declared the Professor, climbing to his feet. "Come along, gentlemen." Umbrella in hand, he strode briskly toward a nearby doorway.

"What's in there?" I asked.

"I haven't the foggiest idea," he said, pushing open the door. M and I glanced at each other, shrugged, and followed him.

If you took an airplane hangar, used dividers to break it into closet-sized cubicles, and put a desk inside each, how many offices would you have? Whatever the answer was, we were looking at it. And I had no doubt that somewhere in the building was a person who not only knew that answer, but had the paperwork to back it up.

A constant stream of pin-striped pedestrians sped around the perimeter of the room, clutching handfuls of paper. The Professor reached out with his umbrella and tapped one on the shoulder as she hurried by. "I say, excuse me—"

"No time," she mumbled, hardly looking up.

He tried another, this one a swarthy man with slicked-back hair. "Sorry, pal," the man said.

"I'm not your pal!" the Professor called after him.

He tried a third, this time reversing his umbrella and using it to hook the person's arm. He pulled his catch to shore, and we saw that it was a pale man with pencil-thin features and a rumpled tie. "Let me go!" the man screeched.

"This will only take a moment," said the Professor.

"I don't have a moment! Do you have any idea how busy I am?"

"Where is the department that handles output passes?" the Professor asked.

"I'm not sure—fifty-sixth, fifty-seventh floor, something like that. I don't have my files with me."

"But the woman downstairs told us to come to this floor," I said.

"Of course she did. All visitors have to come here and fill out a questionnaire. Can I go now?"

"We already filled out a questionnaire," said M.

"I'm talking about the routing questionnaire, not the entry questionnaire," he barked impatiently. "Do you people think you can just waltz in here and get what you want without going through the proper steps?"

"Waltz?" said a voice from behind us. "Why, thank you, I'd love to."

We turned around, and there before us stood living proof that there's an exception to every rule. He was carrying a few sheets of paper, but at that point any resemblance between him and his co-workers ended. He wore a pink shirt, bright green overalls, and Day-Glo tennis shoes. On his head was a beanie with a propeller on it. Just below the propeller was a button with a happy face and the words *Hi! My Name Is Wendell.*

"Pardon me," said the other man, edging backward, "but I'd better go." A few quick steps, and he slipped back into the traffic stream as smoothly as a trout into water.

"Well, if he doesn't want to dance," the newcomer warbled, "then how about you, stranger?" He grabbed the Professor and whirled him around, humming.

"Let go of me this instant!" sputtered the Professor.

"Try not to step on my toes, please," the man said.

The Professor tore himself away and smoothed his clothes. "See here, we don't have time for this kind of nonsense."

"Then let's try another kind—say, charades?"

"Excuse me," I said, "but I couldn't help noticing you're not wearing a suit."

"Neither are you," he said. "I like that." He offered

his hand. "My name is Wendell. Around here, I'm known as Wendell the Wild Man. I never could understand why."

I clasped his hand. There was a loud buzz, and I jumped back.

Wendell giggled in delight and showed us the small, round object he held in his palm. "Pretty swell, huh? Want one?"

"I'll pass, thanks," I said, rubbing my hand.

"If you really work here," said M, "what do you do?"

"As little as possible. Say, how about a round of tic-tac-toe?"

"My good man," said the Professor, "we have more important things on our minds than tic-tac-toe."

"Okay, how about Monopoly?"

The Professor drew himself up to his full height. "As a matter of fact, we're here on a very serious mission. This young man is in need of an output pass."

"Is that all? Why didn't you say so?" Wendell started toward the stream of workers.

Not knowing what else to do, we followed, but as we approached the crowd, I began to feel like a squirrel setting out across an eight-lane highway. "Shouldn't we wait for the light?" I called, but Wendell didn't hear me.

He walked right into the throng, his outfit drawing looks of disgust, and suddenly the sea parted, leaving a path to the other side that would have made Moses proud. Wendell stood in the middle, his propeller spinning, and waved us through like some Technicolor traffic cop. "It pays to be different, I always say," he chortled.

On the other side, he led us through the maze of office

cubicles to a plain, unmarked door. He opened the door and motioned us through.

Amazingly, the second room was as big as the first. But instead of being jammed with cubicles, it was filled to the brim with filing cabinets. The cabinets were stacked from floor to ceiling along the walls, and in rows across the center of the room. There were papers everywhere—strewn on the ground, stuffed between cabinets, hanging from drawers. And yet, for all the mess, there was no sign of people. I asked Wendell why.

"Simple," he replied, his voice echoing off the metal cabinets. "People know that if they came in here, they might actually get something done, and that's the last thing they want to do.

"Let's see," he went on, "they keep output passes around here someplace." He started up one of the aisles, with us close on his heels.

"If it's this easy, why didn't somebody bring us here before?" I asked.

Wendell glanced at the drawer labels as he walked by. "People around here get nervous if they can't give you a form or put you on a waiting list. Me, I'd rather just get things done and go on to the next job."

"Pardon me," said M, "but didn't you say you do as little as possible?"

"Well, sure, but I still get twice as much done as anybody else around here. Why do you think they put up with me?" He found the file he was looking for, pulled out a sheet of paper, and handed it to me.

There was an official-looking stamp at the top, and

under it, written in fancy script, were the words *Output Pass.* Suddenly there was a lump in my throat.

Wendell must have noticed because he said, "Hey, come on, it's only paper."

I shook my head. "It's a lot more than that."

"In that case, take several." Giggling, he pulled out a handful and tossed them into the air.

I stood there watching as they fluttered to the floor like so much confetti. All at once, unable to restrain myself, I dropped down and gathered them up, clutching them to my chest.

When I looked up, Wendell was standing over me, a look of apology on his face. "There's something you should know," he said. "No matter how many passes you have, you won't be able to leave until the bug alert's over."

I sat there, numb, feeling as if I'd been handed a million dollars and then been told it was play money.

The Professor cleared his throat and helped me to my feet. "Then we'll just have to do something about the bug alert. Are there any records on it?"

Wendell led us down a row of cabinets and around a corner. "Welcome to Bug Central," he said, gesturing broadly. Opening a drawer, he flipped through the files, humming as he did. "Ah, yes," he said at last, pulling one out, "here it is." He glanced through its contents. Then he looked up at us, puzzled.

"This may sound funny coming from me," he said, "but there's something strange about this file."

"How so?" I asked.

"Everything about the bug alert has either been cut out or is missing."

There was a noise, and we wheeled to find ourselves face-to-face with the security guard. Wordlessly he took the output passes from me. I was about to launch into a story about how we'd taken a wrong turn on the way to the rest room, when out from behind a bank of files stepped the Computer Police, their crossbows drawn. With them was Delete, an evil grin on her face.

"Gentlemen," she said to the others, "our hunt is over."

The Castle of ROM

I had arrived in CPU City needing just one thing: to get home. In the city, I found I really needed two things: to debug the program and get home. As we left the city the following morning, I realized I now needed three things: to escape Delete, debug the program, and get home. If this was progress, I wanted no part of it.

The Professor, M, and I rode out of the city gates on horseback. I'd gone riding a few times before, but none of the stables had ever asked me to lie bound and gagged across the saddle. I'd have to say that, given a choice, I prefer Western style.

We moved along the bus toward the massive granite cliff atop which the castle of ROM was perched. As we drew closer, the cliff leaned out over us, sucking the sunshine from the landscape and the heat from our bones. Twisting my neck to look at it, I couldn't see how, short of riding in a blimp, we could possibly get to the top. Then, when we were within shouting distance of it, I saw the trail.

Actually, it wasn't a trail so much as a tiny, jagged blemish on the face of the granite. I'm not saying it was narrow, but if you sliced it up into one-inch lengths, you could sell it to Gillette.

The horses had apparently made the climb before, because they started up the cliff, single file, without the slightest hesitation. Once on the trail, it was really no different from a trip to the kitchen for a glass of water—if your faucet were Niagara Falls and you were walking on a tightrope.

Somehow we made it to the top without incident. We rounded a clump of bushes at the trail head, and there before us was the castle of ROM.

Like the cliff, it was solid granite. There was a high wall in front, with turrets at each end and great round towers beyond. Surrounding the structure was a moat whose inky waters rippled with unseen activity.

As we approached, there was a rustling of chains, and the drawbridge was lowered. The police prodded our horses, and, like so many sides of venison, we made our grand entrance into the castle of ROM.

I was hoping to get a better look at the place, but Delete ordered her people to untie us and throw us into the dungeon. As our cell door thudded shut, we heard shouting and the clash of arms.

We rushed over to the dungeon's tiny window, for one giddy moment imagining the Queen and her soldiers riding in to save us. The jousting field below was filled with soldiers, all right—thousands of them—but they weren't with the Queen. These were the King's men, and they were being drilled in the use of weapons. There was something in the scope and mood of the drill that convinced me it wasn't an everyday exercise.

"War," I murmured. "They're preparing for war."

"Good heavens, I think you're right," said the Professor.

"We've got to tell the Queen!" M said.

I watched as the soldiers fired one last volley of arrows into the late-afternoon sky. "What does the King expect to gain by war? We've been to RAM, and there's no sign of the bug there."

"He's a hard man to convince," M replied. "He's sure the Queen's hiding something, and he'll tear the kingdom apart looking for it."

"Come to think of it," I said, "we still haven't seen a sign of the bug anyplace—not even in the files. It's a crazy thought, but could it be there isn't a bug?"

"Interesting idea, Benjamin," said the Professor, "but highly unlikely. If there were no bug, the program would be running normally, and none of this ever would have started."

A short time later, there was a clank, and the door swung open. Two guards strode in and started to lead us away. I asked where we were going.

"I'm afraid it's time for your . . . appointment with Delete," said one of them.

Well, there it was. To be honest, I guess I'd always known that you don't get sucked into a computer and live to tell about it. But I wasn't going to give up without a fight.

"Didn't you know?" I said. "We're here to see the King."

"Nice try," said the guard.

Picking up on my lead, the Professor said. "We've come on a matter of grave urgency. We have a message."

"Oh, yeah?" the man asked. "And who's it from?"

"The Queen," blurted M.

The guard gazed at us coolly. "There are certain things it's not wise to joke about." He cinched the last of our wrists. "Come with me."

"You really should meet the Queen sometime," I said, desperate to stall. "She's beautiful, a real knock-out."

He took one quick step and grabbed me by the front of my shirt. "That's enough," he growled.

Ordinarily I'm not the kind of guy who would press that sort of thing, but this wasn't an ordinary situation.

"A little touchy on that subject, huh?" I said.

He tightened his grip. "I started my career as one of the Queen's guards, right in this castle. She's no longer here, but I won't have her name spoken lightly by someone who never met her."

"But sir," said M, "that's exactly what we're saying— we did meet her, just a microsecond ago."

"If you knew anything about the Queen, you'd know she's been in hiding. You couldn't have met her." He turned toward the door.

"She has blonde hair and green eyes, doesn't she?" I said. The guard stopped. "She loves bits," I went on. "She reads a crystal ball and plays the harp."

"Wait!" cried M. "If you give me my mandolin, I'll play one of her songs."

The man glared at him for several long moments. Finally he nodded to the other guard, who left for a moment and returned with M's instrument. The minstrel tried a few chords and began to play.

It was the song the Queen had sung in the glen, the one about the place of high magic. I remembered the sound of her voice and the way the light filtered through the trees to illuminate her face. As the guard listened, the line of his jaw began to soften. He brushed a hand over his eyes and stared at the floor.

When M finished, the man looked up and said in a low voice, "She used to sing that in her room at night. I'd stand guard in the hallway and listen. I often wondered what the 'place of high magic' would be like to visit, but whatever it's like, I don't think it could be any more magical than that hallway."

He cleared his throat. "I'll take word to the King that you have a message. Of course, I can't promise that he'll want to see you." The two of them left.

"It worked!" I said.

"Yes," said the Professor. "Now instead of being executed before dinner, we'll be executed afterward."

M sat down on a bench, and Negatori jumped into his lap. "We won't be executed at all."

"And how, might I ask, were you able to deduce that?" asked the Professor.

"It's a feeling I have. We'll be fine, Professor."

"That's great, M," I said, "but I'd feel a lot better if we had a plan."

"Bravo, Benjamin," said the Professor. "Logical thinking is our only hope."

Unfortunately, logical thinking is tough when you know your executioner is waiting just around the corner. We huddled and talked things over but didn't come up with anything.

Finally, the cell door opened. We braced ourselves for the bad news.

The guard stepped inside. "The King will see you now," he said.

Benjy Goes for Broke

They took all of us, including Negatori, to a torch-lined chamber. Though apparently intended for large gatherings, the room had just one chair. Situated on a platform several steps above the floor, the chair had immense wooden arms carved in the shape of lions' heads and was upholstered in red fabric laced with gold. In social studies, I'd heard Mrs. Higgenbottom refer to capital cities as *seats of power*. Looking at the King's throne, I could imagine where the expression came from.

We were led to a spot just in front of the platform and told to kneel. From behind a curtain came a procession of courtiers in tunics and brightly colored stockings. I hadn't seen that many tights since the school production of *Swan Lake*.

The courtiers formed two lines leading outward from the throne. Then, as if on cue, they knelt. It was pretty impressive for a spur-of-the-moment ceremony. God knows what they could have put together for a big event like a coronation or bar mitzvah.

The curtain was thrust aside, and out stepped a man wearing a scarlet cape and a massive sword. Tall and broad-shouldered, he moved with the quiet assurance of one to whom power comes naturally. On his head was a crown that glittered with jewels, and beneath the crown was the face I'd seen on a dozen coins. What the coins hadn't revealed, though, was the tension, the impatience, the uneasy expression that shifted as rapidly as storm clouds on a windy day.

The King strode to the throne, swept back his cape, and seated himself. "Cyril," he said to the man on his right, "what do you think of these miserable creatures?"

"They're miserable, sir," Cyril replied breathlessly.

He turned to the woman standing on his left. "And you, Leona, what do you think I should do with them?"

"Well, sir, I suppose you might . . ." she hesitated.

"Release them?" he asked. My heart leaped.

"Yes, sir, that's it—release them," she said, relieved.

"Release them?" he roared. "We capture three glitches, and you want to release them?"

"Well, no, sir . . ." she stammered.

"Pardon me, sir," I said, "but we're not glitches."

Suddenly the room was deathly quiet, and everyone was staring at me. It reminded me of the time I'd come in late for a school assembly. I had to walk all the way up to the first row, and I was wearing brand-new shoes. I won't go into the gory details, but let's just say that for the rest of the semester I was known as Squeaky.

The King lowered his voice in a way that made me wish he'd shouted. "Oh, yes, my young friend," he said, "you are indeed glitches, and in spite of what my learned

76

adviser has just said, you will get—how shall I put it?—the royal treatment." He chuckled, and when he glanced at his advisers, they chuckled along with him.

"With all due respect, sir," said Babbage, showing remarkable tact, "I'd like to point out that we're not just ordinary prisoners. We come with a message from the Queen of RAM."

The King started to snap out an angry response, but with the mention of the Queen's name he caught himself, and his face paled slightly. "Ah, yes," he said. "And what is this so-called message?"

I closed my eyes and prayed that the Professor could invent more than just machines.

"She asks that, whatever your differences, you work with her to achieve peace. She begs that you refrain from violence at all costs."

The King crossed his arms and smiled through clenched teeth. "That's very nice," he said. "And I, in turn, have a message for the Queen. I would tell her this: The Computer Kingdom has had enough peace to last for many lifetimes. The time has come for war."

"Uh, sir, we'd be happy to deliver that message in person," I said.

He walked over to a window that looked out on the jousting field. "I'm sending it in a slightly different form."

The Professor struggled to his feet and started toward the King. "But, Your Highness—"

The guards were on him before he could take another step, one of them encircling his neck from behind and the other holding a sword to his throat.

"Please," begged M, "he didn't mean any harm."

The King strolled slowly over to the Professor and looked him up and down. "Old men do foolish things. Some live to regret it. You, sir, won't have that opportunity." He turned on his heel and walked away.

"The audience," he said, "is over."

If the audience was over, so were our hopes. I wanted desperately to prolong both. "Sir," I called after him, "did it ever occur to you that there might not be a bug?"

The King hesitated. "That, of course, is absurd."

"Maybe it seems like it," I said, "but shouldn't you at least consider the possibility? I mean, look what's at stake. Nobody wants a war."

"That's where you're wrong," he said. "I've been waiting for this chance ever since that addlebrained nincompoop of a Queen left this castle."

The King had no way of knowing it, but he had just revealed the solution to the mystery of the bug.

Choosing my words carefully, I said, "You know, I can sympathize with your situation."

"You can?" he asked.

"Sure. For a while there, it looked like you'd never get your chance to make war on the Queen, right? So you did what any sensible despot would do: You took matters into your own hands and created your own chance."

One of the guards moved toward me, but the King motioned him back. "I suppose I should have your tongue cut out," he said, "but then I'd never find out what I did. Go on."

I'd come too far to back out, and besides, at this point, what did I have to lose? "You say there's a bug in the kingdom, and someone is hiding it. Well, I think you're right. But that someone isn't the Queen."

An excited buzzing broke out in the room. "Silence!" roared the King. In the quiet that followed, he said simply, "Tell me."

I swallowed hard. "That someone is you."

The King's face grew white, then pink, then red. And then a strange thing happened. He threw back his head and whooped with laughter. And when he laughed, everyone laughed. They doubled over and slapped their thighs and howled in merriment, all the while keeping an eye on the King to see what he'd do next.

After a few moments he wiped his eyes, still smiling. "What's your name, boy?"

"Benjamin Bean, sir."

"Benjamin, you just did something that none of my advisers has the courage to do. You stood up to me. I like that. It's one of the few things I miss about not having the Queen around. But," he went on, "as brave as you might be, you're still wrong. And I can prove it." He motioned to one of his aides and whispered something to him. The aide went scurrying off.

The King settled onto his throne, but this time, instead of sitting at rigid attention, he leaned back, crossed his legs, and gazed off into the distance. "I'm the sort of person who needs order in his life. I like to decide on one thing and stick to it. But with the Queen, that was impossible. As soon as we settled on something, she would throw it out and get fresh input. It nearly drove me to distraction. And now in RAM she's gone completely out of control. One nanosecond she's doing word processing, and the next she's playing games! What kind of operation is she running over there?"

M spoke up in a shaky voice. "It seems like a very pleasant place to me, sir."

"Pleasant doesn't run programs. Pleasant doesn't pay the bills."

The aide reentered the room, and behind him strode Delete. She approached the King and bowed her head. "Your Majesty wanted to see me?"

"This young man has accused me of hiding the bug," he said.

"Shall I erase him?" she asked.

"I'd rather you told him why his accusation couldn't possibly be true."

"Of course," she said. "It couldn't be true because I myself saw the bug. The Queen's personal guards keep it with them at all times."

It's called the Big Lie. The idea is that if a false statement is outrageous enough, then people will believe it, figuring you wouldn't dare tell such a whopper. At that moment, I saw that my theory about the bug had been right—to a point. The bug had indeed been hidden and used as an excuse for war, but not by the King.

Delete had done it all.

"Sir," I said to the King, "you said you like people to stand up to you. Well, I'm going to tell you something you probably don't want to hear, but I wish you'd think about it anyway." He nodded.

"My friends and I saw the Queen's guards," I went on, "and they don't have the bug. Neither does the Queen, and as far as we can tell, neither does anyone else in RAM. Not only that, all the records in CPU City that involve the bug have been removed or destroyed."

He raised one eyebrow. "What are you saying?"

"Sir, someone's using your feelings about the Queen to manipulate you for their own purposes. That person is hiding the bug. That person is here in this room."

The King stared at me. His gaze shifted to M, who began to quiver, then to the Professor, whose goatee twitched spasmodically, and finally to Delete. She stared right back at him without saying a word. The woman was cold, calculating, and ruthless, but I had to admit she had guts.

After several moments, the King swiveled slowly around to face us. "I've changed my mind," he said. "Delete won't be erasing you, after all."

The Professor gripped my shoulder in silent congratulations. M grinned unabashedly. "Thank you, sir," he said.

"She won't be erasing you," the King thundered, "because an ordinary execution is too good for you. No, I have another idea.

"Late tomorrow," he said, "my soldiers will invade RAM. Delete has prepared them physically, but I think they could use some psychological preparation as well."

Next to him, Delete smiled and nodded.

The King pointed at us and declared, "Feed them to GIGO the dragon!"

GIGO the Dragon

Our guard escorted us down the hallway past a group of curious onlookers, who were grinning.

"What are they so happy about?" I said.

"Oh, nothing," replied the guard.

"My dear fellow, we may be sentenced to death," said the Professor, "but it's *our* death. We have a right to be told about it."

The guard shrugged. "The fact is that everybody loves watching GIGO. It's kind of like a . . . sport."

"My God," I said. "The Christians and the lions."

"Pardon me?"

"Never mind. It was before your time."

"GIGO—what a strange name," said M.

The guard answered, "It stands for *garbage in, garbage out*—an old folk saying of some kind. Usually GIGO just eats bugs and an occasional insubordinate soldier. But I think the King made an exception in your case because he was so angry."

"And he wants to pump up the troops before going into battle," I said grimly.

The guard nodded and said in a low voice, "I'm sorry things worked out this way. Maybe the King didn't believe your story, but I did. Some of us around here are worried about Delete's power over the King. She seems to bring out the worst in him—not like the Queen."

He took us to a small holding cell, one wall of which was a door made of vertical bars. Through the bars we could see a vast arena surrounded on three sides by a high stone barrier and thousands of empty seats. Inside the arena sat GIGO the dragon.

He looked just about the same as he had in the Queen's crystal ball, only uglier. As big as a two-story house, he was covered with bright purple scales. A row of spines ran down his back and along a gigantic tail. He had webbed feet, knobby knees, and a head the size of a pickup truck. His ears were pointed, and his nostrils could have been fitted with manhole covers. With every breath, puffs of smoke floated from his cavernous mouth.

When the door of our cell clanked shut, GIGO looked up, squinting. "Who's there?" he asked.

I whispered, "He can talk?"

The guard nodded and called out, "It's me, GIGO." Then he turned back to us. "There are a lot of things people don't know about dragons."

"I know you could fit the entire front line of the Pittsburgh Steelers into his mouth," I murmured.

GIGO lurched to his feet and began moving awkwardly around the arena.

"A little clumsy, isn't he?" asked M.

"It's his eyes," the guard said. "Dragons are known

for their weak vision. Don't get your hopes up, though. He can see well enough to . . . get the job done."

"I must say," the Professor commented, "he doesn't look especially vicious."

"He's not, except when there's an audience. That's part of his training."

Sure enough, as soon as the arena doors opened and the soldiers began filling the seats, GIGO planted his feet and sent a tongue of flame arching into the sky. The crowd loved it.

"Tell us more about him," I said, hoping to learn something that might help us. The guard gave me a funny look, and I shrugged. "Morbid curiosity."

"He was found in a nest up in Pascal Peaks," said the guard. "He was brought here as a baby and trained until he was fully grown. That's about all I know."

"It's more than enough, thank you," said the Professor.

Before long the arena was packed, and bloodthirsty shouts echoed off the walls. Compared to these guys, a hockey crowd was like the audience at a flute recital.

"Well," said the guard, "I'm afraid it's time." Without looking at us, he opened the door to the arena and mumbled, "I'm sorry."

M hugged Negatori close and walked through the door. The Professor went right behind him. I took a deep breath and followed.

As we stepped into the arena, a wall of sound hit us. The soldiers, by now whipped to a frenzy, were on their feet, straining to get a look at GIGO's dinner. All in all, I had to believe we were one of the more unusual entrées they'd seen.

"Listen," I shouted to the others, "we've got two things that GIGO doesn't have—vision and mobility. Let's split up and keep moving."

"Keep moving, yes," said M. "Split up, no. We've got to stick together."

"That's illogical!" yelled the Professor in M's face.

"That's tough!" replied M, not budging an inch. The Professor's eyebrows shot skyward, and he backed down.

The floor shook, and I turned to see GIGO the dragon lumbering toward us, his nostrils smoking.

"Sorry, gang," I shouted, "but this meeting is adjourned." We angled across the arena with me in the lead. I've always been fast, especially when chased by dragons.

With a lurch, GIGO changed direction and followed us, nostrils breathing fire, head down, and eyes squinted. He may have been awkward, but those huge legs covered a lot of ground.

The crowd, seeing him gain, screamed. In the first row, the King and Delete sat close together, watching intently.

Just as GIGO was giving new meaning to the expression *hot on the trail,* we hung a quick left. He skidded, hesitated, and finally picked up our path again.

I looked back over my shoulder at the others. "We're doing it!" I called to them, but in that glance I could see that even if I were right, I wouldn't be right for long. The

Professor was struggling to keep up, and M, unable to run freely while he held Negatori, wasn't doing much better.

GIGO was gaining.

The only thing going faster than my legs was my brain, trying desperately to think of a new strategy. Suddenly I had an idea.

"Hurry!" I called to the others. I turned left again, then right, then left and headed for the far wall. They followed, and by the time GIGO realized what had happened, we had picked up valuable ground. We reached the wall while he was still in the middle of the arena.

"Can't keep going much longer," panted the Professor.

"You won't have to," I said quickly. "Just crouch down and stay as still as you can."

The three of us huddled next to the wall. The soldiers, who thought we were giving up, began to boo. GIGO started slowly in our direction, his massive head sweeping back and forth.

"He can't see us!" M whispered.

"Ssh!" said the Professor.

GIGO drew nearer still, searching for some hint of movement or color. As he approached, I noticed a smell that reminded me of a backyard barbecue. I thought of grilled hamburgers and shuddered.

Maybe it was the shudder, or M's green outfit, or the Professor's tall hat. Whatever the cause, GIGO's eyes suddenly focused, and he broke into a transcontinental grin.

"Well, guys," I gulped, "it's been fun."

The soldiers began chanting, "GIGO, GIGO, GI-GO!" In a gesture of triumph, the dragon threw back his head and sent a column of flame into the air. Then he moved toward us.

M stood up and, clutching Negatori to his chest, stepped in front of the Professor and me, shielding us with his body. I grabbed his arm and tried to pull him back, but with a violent twist he wrenched out of my grip.

He looked back at me, and I thought how odd it was that I'd had to go inside a computer to find the best friend I would ever have.

GIGO was right on top of us now, gazing down. He took a deep breath, and I shut my eyes, expecting to hear the roar of a blast furnace.

Instead, I heard a voice that said, "Arnie?"

I opened my eyes. GIGO was bending down, his nose almost touching M, peering intently at Negatori. "Arnie," he said in a hoarse voice, "it's me, GIGO."

Negatori whimpered, his bright eyes blinking, his nose twitching.

Thinking fast, I said, "That's right, GIGO, it's Arnie. We brought him for a visit."

"Who's Arnie?" murmured M.

"I don't know," I whispered back, "but he sounds like my kind of guy."

"Remember, Arn?" GIGO said. "The nest on Pascal Peaks?"

He was treating Negatori like a long-lost brother.

And that's when it hit me: A bit may look nothing like a dragon, but to someone who sees the world through the equivalent of a shower door, a bit might look very much like a dragon egg.

As if from a great distance, the sound of the crowd swept back into my thoughts. The soldiers' chants had turned to cries of rage and frustration.

In their midst, the King huddled with Delete. She rose and shouted some orders, and the next thing we knew, armed soldiers were flooding out onto the arena floor, apparently intent on doing GIGO's job for him. As they closed in on us, the dragon glanced from the soldiers to Negatori and back again.

In that instant GIGO must have come to a decision, because before we knew what had hit us, he'd scooped up Negatori, M, the Professor, and me in one motion and plopped us down just behind his shoulders.

"Hang on, Arnie," yelled GIGO, "we're going home!"

He reared up on his hind legs, and all at once we were two stories off the ground, hanging on for dear life. Below, his great tail curled back on itself, then lashed out at the wall next to us. Rocks went flying in every direction, and a hole appeared. He lashed out again, and the hole grew to the size of a billboard.

Suddenly we were out on the jousting field, moving away from the castle with an army division at our heels. GIGO turned, and I felt his chest expand beneath me. The muscles of his back tensed, and with the roar of a jet airplane, he exhaled, sending a wall of fire racing across the grass between us and our pursuers.

Through the flames, the soldiers watched as GIGO the dragon lumbered across the field and out of the castle grounds.

A Place of High Magic

GIGO's cooking technique may have been sharp, but he'd obviously been neglecting his roadwork. As we moved along a path down the backside of the mountain, he started huffing and puffing almost immediately, and by the time we'd gone the equivalent of ten miles or so, he sounded like a candidate for a very large iron lung.

"Rest," he said, "gotta rest." We saw no reason to put up an argument, since it was getting dark. Come to think of it, we saw no reason to put up an argument, period.

M, the Professor, and I wanted desperately to get to RAM and warn the Queen about the attack, but there would have been no point in taking off on foot when we had at our disposal the world's only purple, fire-breathing taxi. Even stopping for the night, we could get to RAM faster on GIGO's back. Of course, GIGO might not want to go to RAM, but as long as he took us as far as Pascal Peaks, we'd still end up ahead.

We found a big cave that suited our needs perfectly. GIGO, whose night vision was even worse than his day vision, ran into a wall, tripped over a boulder, collapsed on the ground, and fell asleep before we'd had time to climb off his back.

The guard had said there were a lot of things people didn't know about dragons. We were about to find out one more thing: Dragons snore.

Don't try to tell me the night lasted less than a millionth of a second. It was at least two weeks later when the sun finally climbed over the horizon and shone into the cave, revealing M, the Professor, and me staring red-eyed at the ceiling.

GIGO sputtered and coughed and heaved himself upright. "Arnie?" he wheezed.

"Well," I said quickly, "time to hit the road, huh?"

"Where's my brother?"

Nearby, under M's cape, a bit-sized lump quivered. "He's had a pretty hard night," said M.

"I want to see Arnie!" GIGO roared, his face twisted into a scowl. Apparently he wasn't a morning person.

M and I exchanged glances, then M picked up Negatori and walked slowly toward GIGO. As he did, the lines on the dragon's face softened.

"Hi, Arn," said GIGO. He leaned down to get a better look. As luck would have it, that's just what he got.

"That's not Arnie!" bellowed GIGO, sending a tongue of flame shooting just past M's shoulder. "You lied to me!"

"That's not precisely true," the Professor pointed out in an unsteady voice. "We simply didn't—"

"I'm mad!" yelled the dragon. "I'm very mad!"

You had to admire the guy's forthright style. He advanced, his nostrils doing a nifty imitation of Chevy exhaust pipes. We edged away until our backs were quite literally to the wall. Unless we did something fast, we were faced with the prospect of becoming an oversized shish kebab.

"I can understand how you feel," I said, trying a ploy I'd once heard a child psychiatrist use. "Why don't we sit down and talk about it?"

"You lousy bums!" cried GIGO. I can't say I was surprised he ignored the ploy. It hadn't worked on me either.

"You bums!" he repeated, moving steadily forward, his voice growing shriller. "Bums!" he yelled again, his voice and his stride breaking at the same time.

Before our eyes, GIGO the dragon plopped down in a heap and began to cry.

That's when M did one of the bravest things I've ever seen. He handed Negatori to me, then walked over to GIGO and began petting the top of one gigantic foot.

The dragon looked up, his eyes filled with tears. "I'm tired of fighting. I told them that, but they wouldn't listen."

"We'll listen," said M.

"You will?"

"Sure. What would you like to do?"

GIGO thought for a minute. "Go home?"

"Then that's what you should do," said M.

"Is Arnie there?" GIGO asked.

"I bet he might be."

GIGO wiped his eyes. "Okay, then."

"Do you think we could get a ride as far as the mountains?'' asked M. In response, GIGO picked us up, one by one, and carefully placed us on his shoulders.

It wasn't the most comfortable ride in the world, but it was fast. Once we got onto the open road, GIGO established a lopsided gait that ate up distance the way he'd once eaten up . . . well, never mind. He must have gotten a good night's sleep, because fatigue wasn't nearly the problem it had been before. We only had to stop a few times, and at each stop he was ready to go again in no time.

By midmorning we were at the base of Pascal Peaks, and GIGO, his eyes riveted to the mountaintops, had quite literally dropped us off. We barely had enough time to get back on our feet and shout a quick goodbye before he charged up into the foothills and disappeared from sight.

GIGO the dragon was going home.

It was just a short walk to Memory Lane. We hurried up the path and climbed the ridge overlooking RAM. We reached the top, expecting the same pastoral scene that had greeted us before. We were greeted, all right— like a slap across the face.

RAM was at war.

A contingent of the King's soldiers must have ridden all night on horseback, hoping to beat us to the Queen and thus retain the element of surprise. The citizens of RAM, caught unprepared, had thrown up a barrier of logs and stones around the Queen's mansion and were trying desperately to hold off the invaders. It appeared that the assault would already have succeeded if it hadn't been for the data, who had left their tents and were hurling themselves at the attackers from one side. The soldiers, obviously instructed not to harm the program, were trying in effect to shield themselves with one hand and fight with the other.

M looked down on the battle, his face as ravaged as the landscape before us. "We failed the Queen," he said miserably. I couldn't disagree.

"This is catastrophic!" said the Professor. "Not only will RAM be damaged physically, but if the King's forces win, the balance of power between RAM and ROM will be completely upset. The computer may never function properly again."

"I can't just stand here and watch," said M. "I'm going down there to fight."

"Gentlemen," declared the Professor, "what the Queen needs is not our physical but our mental powers. In a word, logic.

"We've said from the first," he explained, "that we could stop this war by locating the bug and correcting it, thus enabling the program to run again. That's still true even though the fighting has begun, correct?" We nodded.

"All right, then," he continued, "we know from what the King told us that most of his army won't arrive before late this afternoon. And from the looks of things, this first wave of attackers can't win the war by themselves."

"Great," I said. "So we have until tonight to hitch a ride back to ROM, find the bug, and spring it loose."

"Ah," he replied, "but this is where logic comes in. What makes you think the bug is in ROM?"

"Delete's got it," I said. "Where else would she keep it?"

"But, Benjy," said M, "she wouldn't want it anywhere near the castle because the King might run across it."

"Precisely," declared the Professor. "Now, I maintain that if we simply use our powers of reason, we should be able to make an accurate guess as to the bug's true location."

"Delete would want it someplace out of the way," I said.

The Professor shook his head. "Then it would be out of the way for her, too. No, Benjamin, I think what we're looking for is a location closer at hand, but perhaps where people seldom go."

"The Arithmetic-Logic Unit!" said M. "It's run by the priests of the Logical Order."

"Of course!" exclaimed the Professor. "She could have forced the priests to create the bug, then hold it prisoner. As soon as RAM was defeated, she could quickly restore the bug's original value, causing the program to run once again, and the King would be given credit for saving the kingdom."

"And the worst part," said M, "is that the King would believe it."

The Professor looked at M with new respect. "You see," he said, "logic is not a religion, but a tool."

I looked at the valley below. "I hate to interrupt, guys, but the Queen's still in trouble down there. What do you say we pack up our toolbox and get going, huh?"

Surrounded by shade trees and built of stone, the Arithmetic-Logic Unit, called the ALU, was an island of antiquity in the metal-and-plastic world of CPU City. Once in a while, a priest wearing a hooded robe would cross the courtyard in front, but otherwise the place was completely still.

We watched from across the street, crouched behind an office building, where we had stopped to devise our strategy and eat. Noticing that M had hardly touched his food, I asked if he was all right.

"I'm fine, I suppose," he said. "But I was just thinking that while you're looking around the ALU, maybe I should stay here and stand guard."

"This is no time to change our plans," snapped the Professor. "Besides, you're the one who said we should stick together."

"That place makes you nervous, doesn't it?" I asked M.

He hung his head. "I know that to you it's just a bunch of buildings, but to data like me it's scary. When we go in there, we usually come out changed into something different."

" 'A place of high magic,' " I murmured. He nodded.

"There's nothing magical about it!" said the Professor. "The data are taken through some simple, logical steps, and unless you go through those steps, you will, I regret to say, remain exactly as you are." M didn't look convinced.

"You know," I told him, "I always felt nervous, too, but not just about the ALU. The whole computer bothered me. But I've noticed that the more time I spend inside it, the less nervous I feel. Maybe the same thing will happen to you."

M thought about it for a moment, then picked up Negatori. "I guess I'll give it a try," he said, holding the little bit close.

According to plan, we made our way around the side of the ALU to an area dense with shrubbery. From there, we sneaked up to a window and looked inside.

It appeared to be a library. The walls were covered with leather-bound books, and a few men and women in robes sat at tables studying. We moved down to the next window and saw a deserted chapel. The next room was obviously a dormitory, and next to that, a woodworking shop and a meeting hall. As we moved from window to window around the perimeter of the U-shaped building, we saw other priests going about their daily activities, but nothing at all suspicious and certainly nothing resembling a bug.

"Maybe we were wrong," M whispered.

The Professor looked up at the sun, which was about to dip below the treetops. "The rest of the King's army is about to reach RAM. We can't afford to be wrong."

"But if the bug's here," I said, "why isn't there any sign of it—like guards, for instance?"

"There will be," he said, his jaw set firmly.

The next window opened into a large dining hall, where a man in a white apron and hat was preparing place settings for what looked like a banquet. At the head table was a particularly lavish setting decorated with tapestries and flowers, apparently for a special guest.

The man in the apron finished and moved toward one

of the doors. We shuffled over to an adjacent window just in time to see him enter the kitchen. There were wonderful-looking soups and meats and vegetables on the stove. Next to me, Negatori's sniffer was going a mile a minute, but I didn't give the food more than a quick glance. What really caught my eye was slouched in a chair in the corner, fast asleep.

It was one of the Computer Police. On the floor next to him were his crossbow and sword.

"There's your guard," said the Professor, "if you could call him that."

The cook ladled some stew into a bowl and set it on a tray, which he picked up. He said something to the guard, who awoke with a start, adjusted his armor, and followed the cook out of the kitchen, leaving his weapons behind.

Wasting no time, the Professor opened the window, and we dropped to the floor. Wordlessly he directed us to pick up the guard's weapons; then he peeked out the door and motioned for us to follow.

We went through the door and into the central courtyard, which was empty. Ahead of us, the cook and guard were just disappearing through an archway leading to the back. We hurried after them, crouching low to avoid being seen.

They took a path that led through some trees to a small wooden shack with no windows. The guard unlocked the door and waited outside while the cook went in. A moment later, the cook reappeared minus the tray, backing away and gesturing the way I've seen my mom do when she's trying to escape a door-to-door salesman.

The guard closed the door firmly and locked it, then grinned at the cook, who was smiling and shaking his head.

They walked off, leaving us alone with—did we dare imagine it?—the bug.

"This is too easy," I said.

"I hate to sound negative," said M, "but that door looks pretty sturdy, and we don't have a key."

"My dear fellow," declared the Professor, "if you'd been paying attention when we met, you'd remember that among my inventions was a method for picking locks."

We hurried over to the shack, where the Professor reached up and pulled a straight pin from the crown of his hat, then knelt and begin fiddling with the lock. As he worked, we heard a muffled male voice inside.

"What's he saying?" I asked M.

"I don't know, but it almost sounds like he's laughing."

M was right. Between sentences there were high-pitched giggles. I shrugged. "I guess if you're a prisoner you might as well enjoy yourself."

I glanced uneasily toward the main building, then down at the Professor. "How's it coming?"

"Patience, Benjamin, patience." He slid the pin sideways, then rotated it once. There was a click, and he looked at us, beaming. "Genius triumphs again." He got to his feet and opened the door.

A red-and-white polka-dot five stood on the other side. "Knock, knock," he said.

"I beg your pardon?" said the Professor.

"You're supposed to say 'Who's there?' " replied the five.

"My dear fellow, we've come to rescue you."

"Come on, it won't take long."

"This is preposterous!" the Professor declared.

"Okay," I said to the five, "who's there?"

"Sid."

"Sid who?"

"Siddown and make yourselves comfortable," he hooted. "Great, huh?"

M cocked his head sideways. "Have we met someplace before?" he asked.

"Be-four?" said the prisoner, elbowing the Professor. "Don't you mean be-five?"

"You know," I said, "somehow you do seem familiar. I wonder . . . wait a second! You're Mark!"

"Get set, go!" He shook with laughter.

"The Marks Brothers!" said M. "They said their brother had disappeared."

"Great Scott," said the Professor, "you're right! Delete must have kidnapped him and changed him into a five."

"Actually," said Mark, "I didn't really mind it. Gave me a chance to work on my solo act."

"But, Professor," I said, "changing one little quotation mark wouldn't bring down the entire program, would it?"

"To the contrary, Benjamin. Any mistake, no matter how minor, can render a program useless. In point of fact, entering one quotation mark without its twin is one of the most common errors in programming. You see—"

He was interrupted by the sound of hoofbeats coming from the front of the ALU. Negatori sat up straight, and the rest of us exchanged worried glances.

"I'm going to look," I said. I sneaked back through the trees to the archway and peered into the courtyard.

The banquet's guest of honor had arrived. It was Delete.

Bug and Debug

As Delete and her escorts made their way to the banquet hall, I hurried back and told the others.

"Quickly, there's no time to lose!" the Professor said. "Mark, where did they change you into a five?"

"Back there," he said, pointing to a grove of trees behind us.

"Then follow me," said the Professor, setting off toward the trees.

Deep in the grove was a metal vault the size of a house. It appeared to be deserted, but to be safe, the rest of us stayed out of sight while the Professor cautiously approached the place, carrying the sword in one hand and his umbrella in the other. He crouched in front of the entrance, pulled the pin from his hat, and began jiggling it in the lock. A moment later, he was peering through an open door, checking for more guards. He motioned for us to join him.

We found him standing inside, gazing with pride and wonder at the scene before him. "Magnificent!" he breathed.

From outside it had looked like a low, one-level building. It was in fact a ten-story skyscraper, nine stories of which were underground. The interior consisted of one very tall room whose walls were lined from top to bottom with circuit boards. The floor of the room was divided into two parts: one, a labyrinth of convoluted passageways connected by gates; the other, a series of massive instrument panels that made the controls of a DC-10 look like a Model T dashboard.

We were at the very top of the room, on a walkway that ran around the perimeter. Standing on one side of me was M, who seemed to have taken quivering lessons from Negatori. On the other side was Mark. "Anybody got a water balloon?" he asked, leaning out over the railing.

"They can call the other building whatever they like," declared the Professor, "but this is the real Arithmetic-Logic Unit. The gates on the first floor are called logic gates. Put very simply, when a byte of data such as Mark goes through one of them, his value is changed."

"You know," commented Mark, "I've always said that my bark is worse than my byte." He elbowed me, chuckling.

The Professor handed the sword to M and grabbed Mark by one ear. "Come along now," he said, hustling the polka-dot comedian over to a nearby stairway.

"What about us?" M called after him, dangling the sword between his thumb and finger the way you might hold a dead mouse.

"Watch for trouble," the Professor shouted back.

Negatori took a couple of quick laps around the walkway while M and I set up our lookout. M, sword in hand, stationed himself just outside the entrance. I took the crossbow to a spot by the railing where I could watch both the door and the action below.

The Professor arrived at the bottom floor and began studying the vast instrument panels. Mark stood behind him, trying out jokes and practicing his soft shoe. After just a few moments, the Professor reached out and pushed a button.

Bingo.

The panels lit up like a high-tech Christmas tree, and the building began to vibrate. Across the walkway, Negatori jumped straight up in the air and started running in circles.

"Quickly," the Professor yelled to Mark, "go to the gates!"

"Hey, Professor," he replied, "why did the nibble cross the road?"

"Just go!"

There was a tap on my shoulder. It was M. His face was the color of guacamole. "Someone's coming," he said in a pinched voice.

I went to the door and looked. There was movement beyond the trees, and voices. I strained to see who the new arrivals were, and suddenly they had entered the grove and were charging straight toward us.

At the front of the group were two of the Computer Police, their swords drawn. Behind them, a black scowl on her face, strode Delete.

"Time to close up shop," I said. I heaved the door

shut, then locked and bolted it. "Hurry up, Professor," I called, "we've got visitors."

An instant later, we heard the rattling of a key in the lock. The knob turned, but the bolt held.

"Now what do we do?" asked M.

"Pray that two people know what they're doing—the Professor and the guy who made that bolt."

There was an ominous pause, then the voice of Delete. Oddly, it carried none of the strident quality we'd heard before. Instead, it was husky, almost soothing. "Benjamin Bean?" I kept quiet and waited. "Benjamin, there's been a misunderstanding. We realize now that you meant no harm. The King has authorized me to clear you and your friends of all charges."

"The King doesn't even know you're here," I said. "The only thing he's authorized you to do is destroy RAM, and we intend to see that that never happens."

When she replied, there was steel in her voice. "Open the door, Benjamin Bean. Compared to my wrath, the flames of GIGO will seem like a breath of spring."

"Go home, Delete," I said. "Your plan failed."

"Perhaps your minstrel friend will listen," she shot back. "Ask him what instrument he'll play when his hands have been chopped off. Ask him what songs he'll sing when his tongue has been ripped out."

M looked down at his hands, blinking rapidly. "You okay?" I asked him. He took a deep breath and nodded.

Outside, Delete called to her men: "Break down the door!" Silence. "I said break down the door! There's nothing to be afraid of—it's just a building."

105

Over the hum of the machinery, I heard the Professor barking instructions to Mark. I wondered how he'd feel about getting an assist from his lifelong enemy, superstition.

"All right, then," shouted Delete, "I'll do it myself."

A few moments later, something heavy slammed against the door. I remembered the big logs I'd seen lying in the grove and tried to imagine anybody but Delete lifting one single-handedly.

"Stand back by the railing," I told M. I called down below, "We may not be able to hold them much longer."

"Please, Benjamin, try!" replied the Professor, working frantically at one of the panels.

There was a crash, and the door bulged toward us. Across the walkway, Negatori skittered for cover.

"Wait, I've got it!" shouted the Professor. He threw a switch, then pressed a series of buttons. A green light began to blink. "Mark, go through the first gate!" he said.

M and I looked on tensely as Mark tap-danced his way through the opening. There was a flash of light, and suddenly he was no longer a red-and-white polka-dot five. He was a red-and-white polka-dot four.

"Hey, Doc, that was some diet!" he called out.

"Confound it!" bellowed the Professor, turning back to the panel.

Behind us, there was another crash. The bolt exploded off its hinges, and we found ourselves face-to-face with Delete. She let go of the log, and it hit the ground with a dull thud.

"Hello, my friends," she purred.

As she drew her sword, I positioned myself in front of M, holding my crossbow at the ready. "One move, and you're Swiss cheese," I said, trying to keep my voice from shaking.

"No, Benjamin Bean," she said, a faint smile on her lips. "I don't think so."

I tried to answer, but my mouth didn't cooperate. For some reason, I found myself staring into her eyes. They were remarkable when you stopped to look at them. They weren't brown or blue or green, but absolute pitch-black. It was almost as if they weren't eyes at all, but holes through which you could see into the farthest reaches of space, where there were no stars or planets or people or problems. There was nothing at all.

"Benjy, look away!" M yelled.

I collapsed in sections to the ground. Something was going wrong, but I couldn't for the life of me decide what.

I watched, fascinated, as Delete swiveled her head toward M. Gripping his sword in both hands, he turned away, trying not to meet her gaze, but he kept being drawn back as if by a magnet. Finally he couldn't resist any longer, and he looked directly into Delete's eyes.

I started to shout a warning. It was like trying to talk after getting a filling at the dentist. "No, M, don' looh," I called out, my lips slapping together like a pair of winter mittens. He didn't hear me.

I tried to lift the crossbow, but it might as well have been a city bus. I shook my head, hoping to clear out the cobwebs, and things came into sharper focus. Dragging myself to the top of the staircase, I looked down below, where the Professor was pushing buttons and gesturing, all the while shouting instructions to Mark.

I turned back to M and was dismayed to see him staring intently at Delete. I waited for his eyes to sag shut, but instead, they grew wider and began to glisten. His face, meanwhile, was turning a deeper green, the green of moss and pine trees and alpine forests, and it seemed to me that somehow it had actually started to glow. Delete gazed right back at him, her eyes squinted in concentration. And then an amazing thing happened.

Delete flinched.

In that instant, the Professor's voice rang out: "I've almost got it!"

Raising her sword, Delete took one quick step in M's direction, then veered off. Suddenly I was the only thing between her and the staircase. She lunged to one side of me, next to the railing. I thought of the Professor and M and the Queen and the rolling fields of RAM. Then, with all the strength I could muster, I lifted my two-ton foot and stuck it right in her path.

It all seemed to take place in slow motion. She looked at my foot. Her mouth twisted into an awful grimace. She planted her boot firmly on the ground. She sprang high into the air, trying to jump over the obstacle. On the way up, her toe caught the top of my shoe. Her arms flailed. The light flickered off her sword. And, with an unearthly screech, Delete sailed out over the railing like a huge black bird.

"Done!" cried the Professor from below. I looked down just in time to see him rush over and embrace the result of his labors, a pink quotation mark with a straw hat and a silly grin.

In the space the Professor had just vacated, Delete crashed, arms outspread, onto one of the instrument panels. There was a deafening explosion, and when the smoke cleared, we were looking at a mass of twisted metal—but no Delete.

We never learned for sure what happened to her. But I had a hunch about it. I figured she'd gone back to the cold and lonely place I'd seen when I peered into her eyes. What she'd left on the instrument panel was, when you stopped to think about it, both the essence of her character and a fitting legacy.

Nothing.

Home

I raced through the streets of CPU City, with M and the Professor struggling to keep up.

"I say," panted the Professor, "where are we going?"

"And why are we in such a big hurry to get there?" said M.

"You'll see," I replied.

We had come from the Arithmetic-Logic Unit, where we had waited through the night to receive news from RAM. As the sun rose, word had come at last: The King, upon learning of Delete's treachery, had called off his attack and agreed to a peace conference with the Queen.

My companions, jubilant, felt they deserved a rest, and I couldn't blame them. The Professor had saved his computer. M had been part of momentous events and was already planning songs to commemorate them. We had accomplished all that we'd set out to do—except for one minor detail, roughly the size of Mount Everest.

We turned a corner and found ourselves in front of the massive Control Unit building. I led the way inside and went to the front desk, where we found the same woman in the same chair wearing the same frown.

"Fill these out, please," she intoned, handing us a set of entry questionnaires.

"We'd like to see Wendell," I said.

Her already frigid gaze sprouted a new set of icicles. "The worker you refer to is no longer employed here."

I felt a chill, and all at once I was sure Wendell had lost much more than his job. I stepped back, staggered by the thought that it had been my fault.

After a moment, I gathered my wits and, determined not to let anything stop me, asked, "Who do I see about getting an output pass?"

"Just fill these out, please," she repeated.

How do you reason with a tape recorder? We did as she said and were sent once again to the thirty-seventh floor. From there we went to the twelfth floor, then the ninth, then the forty-second. By the time the Control Unit closed down at the end of the afternoon, we were convinced we'd seen everything in the building *but* an output pass.

"Come back tomorrow," said a man at the front door, locking it behind us.

"Count on it," I muttered.

As we walked away, I was struck once again by the immaculate condition of CPU City and found myself longing for the familiar clutter of my bedroom at home. I thought of the dust balls under my bed and felt a surge of warmth. I yearned for the sight of an empty soda can, a wad of paper, a dirty window.

And then, suddenly, I saw one. The glass on a store-front window was spotted and cracked, and through the dirt I could read the word BOUTIQUE.

Without thinking, I said, "Let's go in there."

The shop was wonderful; it was as filthy as the window. The proprietor, his back to us, was off in one corner arranging a rack of brightly colored clothes. His purple velour jumpsuit was a tip-off, but it was the beanie that gave him away.

"Wendell!" I shouted.

He turned around. "You're back!" he cried, racing across the room and giving me a big hug. "I was afraid you'd been erased."

"I thought they'd done the same to you," I said.

"Me?" he said. "Never." He told us how he'd been fired, and we filled him in on all that had happened to us.

"Heroes!" he said, when we were finished. "I've got heroes in my store!"

"We cost you your job," I said. "How can you call us heroes?"

"That wasn't a job; it was a sentence. Now, this"—he gestured at the multicolored mess around him— "this is what I call a job."

"How's business?" asked M.

"Terrible," Wendell replied with a giggle, "but who cares? I'm happy, and I owe it all to you."

Emboldened, I ventured, "Do you still know anyone over at the Control Unit?"

"Are you kidding?" he said. "They think I'm crazy."

My spirits sagged. "So I guess you don't know how I can get another output pass."

"I didn't say that," he replied. He threw on a raccoon coat and started for the door. "Follow me."

A moment later, we were standing at a side entrance to the Control Unit. Wendell fished a ring of keys out of his pocket. "I never did turn these in," he said. "Too many forms to fill out." He unlocked the door, and we went inside.

We took a freight elevator to the thirty-seventh floor, where another key got us into the familiar storage room stacked high with filing cabinets.

"When Delete arrested you, she took all the output passes," Wendell said. Then he grinned slyly. "At least, that's what she thought."

He led us to an especially decrepit bank of cabinets off in one corner and opened a drawer. "I always kept an extra pass stashed away here in the history section. Let's see now," he said, thumbing through a sheaf of documents, "it should be here someplace."

"History?" crowed the Professor. "Then surely there's some mention of me." He pulled out another drawer and began ransacking the files.

"Found it!" cried Wendell, handing me a sheet of paper.

Written at the top of the page were two words which, despite anything the Professor might say, were magical: *Output Pass.*

M put his hand on my shoulder and squeezed. "You're almost home, Benjy."

"Wendell," I said, cradling the paper as if it were the original Declaration of Independence, "how can I thank you?"

"Just enjoy yourself," he replied, smiling, "no matter which peripheral you go to."

"Peripheral?" asked M. "What do you mean?"

Wendell beamed. "This pass will take Benjy to any peripheral village he chooses—Keyboard, Joystick, Printer, or Monitor."

"But didn't you know?" I said. "I need to go farther than that."

Before Wendell could reply, the Professor fumed, "Blast it all, these files are a mess! I can't find the B's!" He slammed a drawer shut.

All the filing cabinets along the wall began to sway.

"They're going to fall!" yelled Wendell. "Everybody, run for it!"

As we took off down the aisle, I glanced over my shoulder and saw the cabinets doing a slow-motion mambo. And I saw something else: Negatori was asleep on the floor right in their path.

I did an about-face and ran back. I scooped up the little bit and headed for the doorway where the others stood, out of danger. I could see that the cabinets had started their final downward plunge. It was going to be close.

"Hurry, Benjy!" cried M. In my arms, Negatori whimpered frantically.

The cabinets were right on top of me. I tossed Negatori into M's waiting arms, then summoned my last ounce of strength and dove.

There was a sharp pain, and the dim light of the storage room flickered out.

Two shadowy figures bent over me. "Benjy?" said a male voice.

"M, is that you?" I answered.

"No, Benjy, it's me."

The place grew brighter, and a face came into focus. It was Dexter. Peering over his shoulder, silhouetted against a ceiling covered with cobwebs, was Velma. "You really threw a scare into us," she said.

I raised my head. "Where's M? Where's the Professor, and Wendell?"

"Huh?"

"You know—the Computer Kingdom."

Velma cocked one eyebrow and glanced at Dexter. "He must have really gotten a jolt."

"You reached behind the computer and touched a cable," Dexter told me, "and the next thing we knew, you were out cold. It must have been an electrical shock."

"When did all this happen?" I asked.

"Just a second ago."

"That long, huh?" I climbed unsteadily to my feet, with Dexter supporting me. "Did you see me get sucked inside the computer?"

"Benjy," said Velma gently, "all this stuff you're talking about—it must have been a dream."

The Computer Kingdom a dream? Was it possible? I remembered wondering how medieval England, a Victorian gentleman, and a frightened eleven-year-old boy could end up inside a computer, and suddenly the whole thing seemed preposterous. Well, not the whole thing.

115

There was always M. There would always be M.

"What were you saying a minute ago?" asked Dexter. "You know, about a computer place?"

I started to describe the land of bits and bytes and polka-dot comedians, but somehow I didn't feel like talking about it. "Could I sit down?" I said.

Dexter guided me to the chair in front of his computer, and as he did, he glanced at the monitor. "I've still got to debug that program," he said.

"Check your quotation marks," I said without thinking. "You may be missing one."

He studied the screen. "You're right," he said, after several seconds. "How'd you know that?"

"Nothing mysterious about it," I replied. "Just good old-fashioned logic."

Dexter made a few quick corrections, and moments later the program was up and running. "Here's that list of books on Charles Babbage. Boy, it's two pages long —he must have really been something."

"Nice guy," I said. "Kinda cranky, though. Not like M."

"Benjy," asked Velma, "are you okay?"

"Yeah, fine."

I guess when all was said and done, I'd gotten what I wanted: I was back outside the box, peering in. After all the times I'd looked forward to this moment, I found myself having a very strange reaction.

I felt sad.

"Well, young man," said Velma, "I think maybe you need some rest. How about I drive you home?"

I watched as Dexter leaned over and tapped out a series of commands on the keyboard.

"You know, Velma," I said, scooting my chair closer to the computer, "if it's okay with you, I think I'll stick around for a while."

About the Author

"When I first began reading about computers, I had a terrible time remembering all the parts," says author RONALD KIDD. "So I dreamed up a land, the Computer Kingdom, in which the parts were places and the data were rainbow-colored characters who ran around singing songs and having adventures and telling bad jokes. Somehow that made the terms easier to remember and a lot more fun."

A writer and producer of educational programs, Ronald Kidd lives in Altadena, California. He is the author of four other juvenile novels, most recently *Sizzle & Splat.*